# HAYLEE AND COMET

## Over the Moon

# DEBORAH MARCERO

Roaring Brook Press
New York

To the dear friends that stay,
long after we part. —DM

Published by Roaring Brook Press
Roaring Brook Press is a division of Holtzbrinck Publishing Holdings Limited Partnership
120 Broadway, New York, NY 10271 • mackids.com

Library of Congress Control Number: 2021046005
ISBN 978-1-250-77441-5

Our books may be purchased in bulk for promotional, educational, or business use.
Please contact your local bookseller or the Macmillan Corporate and Premium Sales Department
at (800) 221-7945 ext. 5442 or by email at MacmillanSpecialMarkets@macmillan.com.

First edition, 2022 • Book design by Kirk Benshoff and Sunny Lee

The art for this book was rendered with ink, colored pencils, watercolor, gouache,
and acrylic paint on hot press watercolor paper.

Printed in China by Toppan Leefung Printing Ltd., Dongguan City, Guangdong Province

1   3   5   7   9   10   8   6   4   2

# The Letter

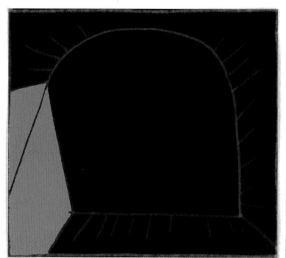
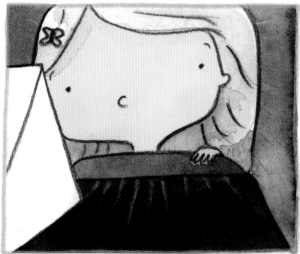

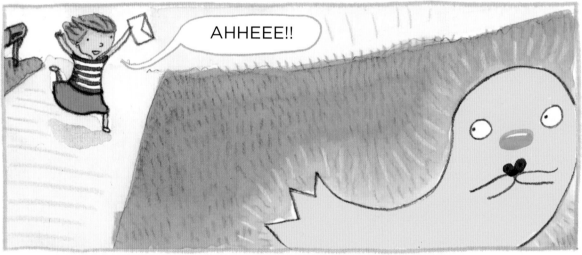

AHHEEE!!

A letter! A letter!

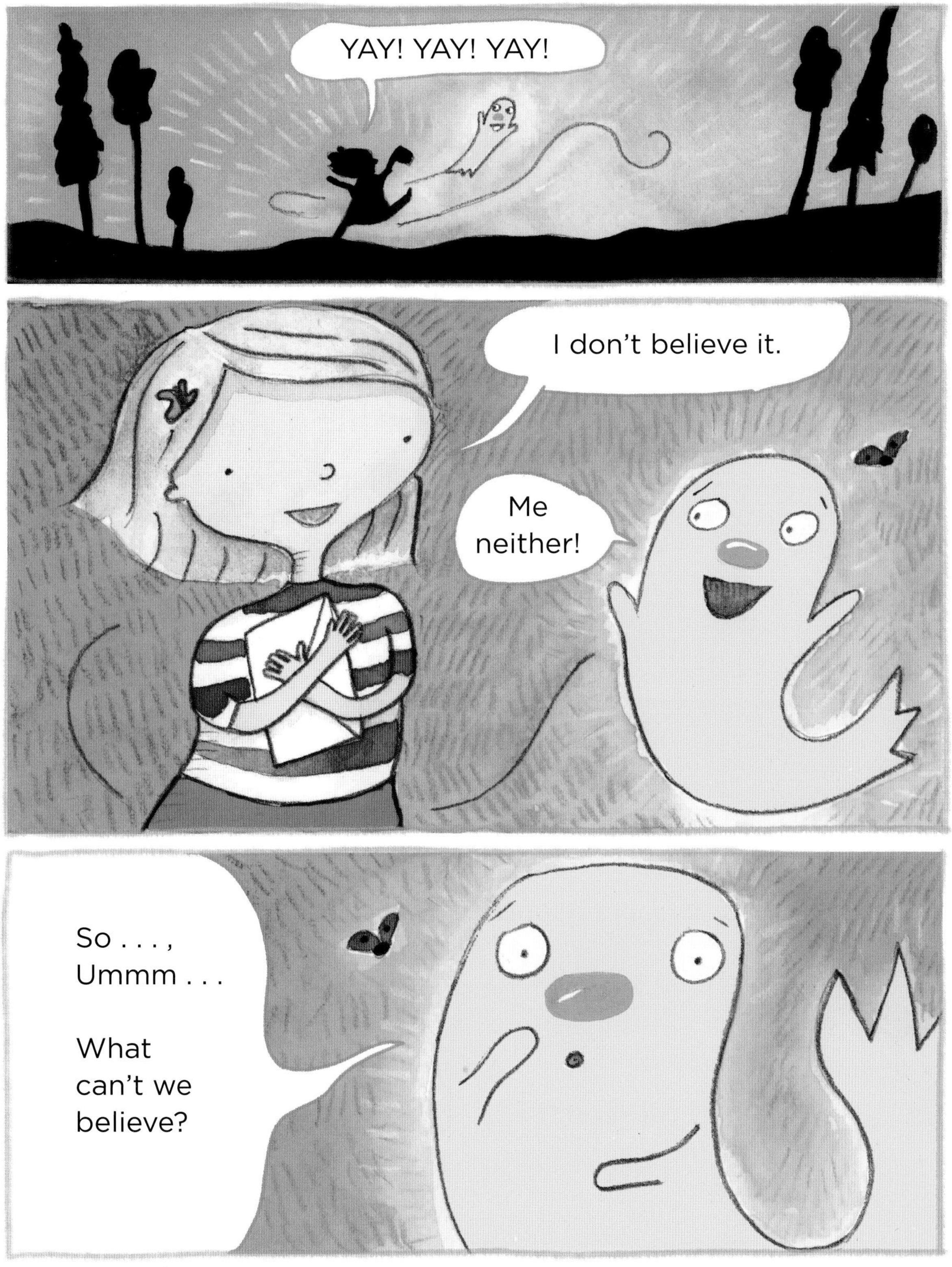

YAY! YAY! YAY!
I don't believe it.
Me neither!
So . . . , Ummm . . .
What can't we believe?

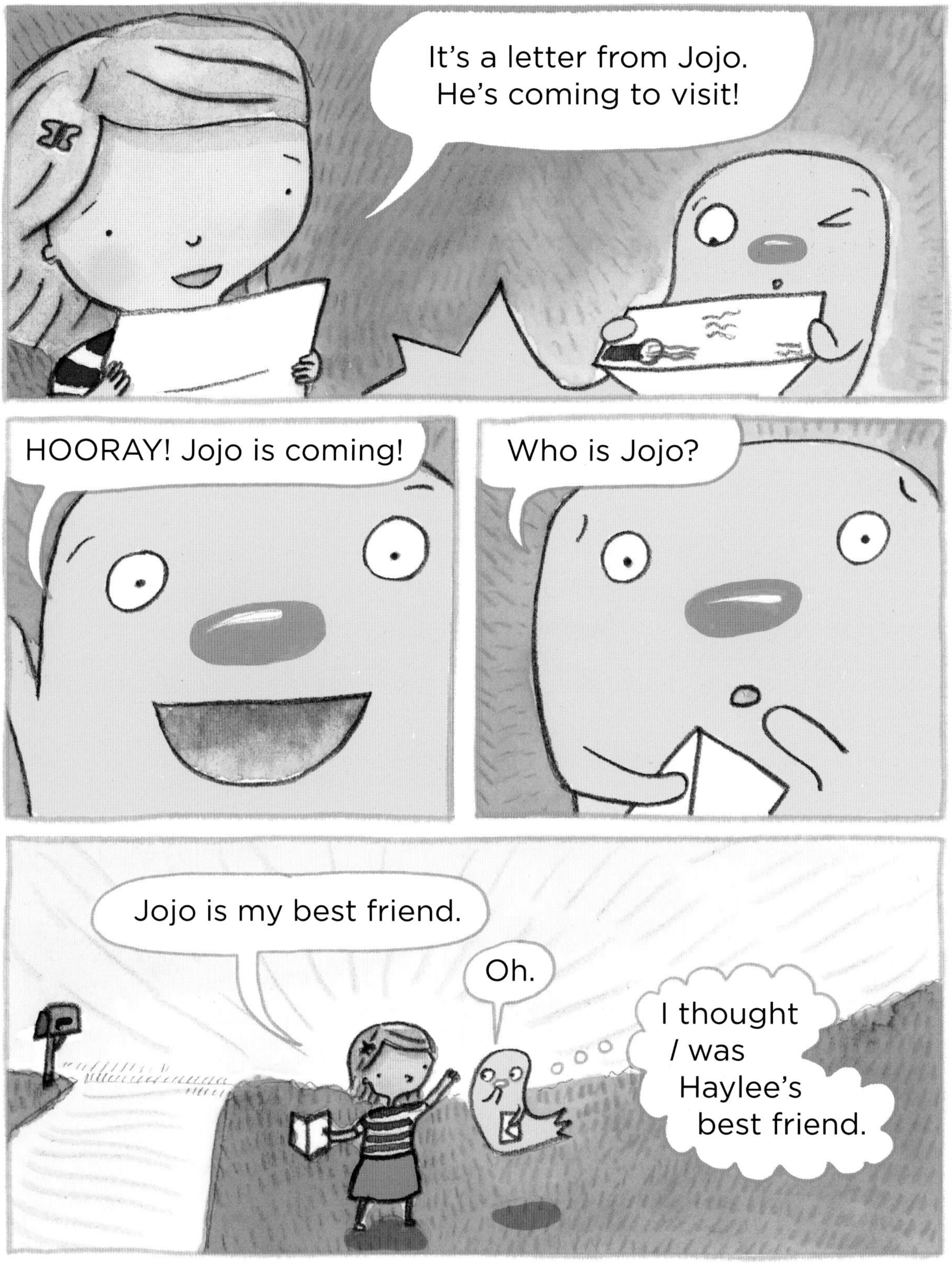
It's a letter from Jojo. He's coming to visit!
HOORAY! Jojo is coming!
Who is Jojo?
Jojo is my best friend.
Oh.
I thought I was Haylee's best friend.

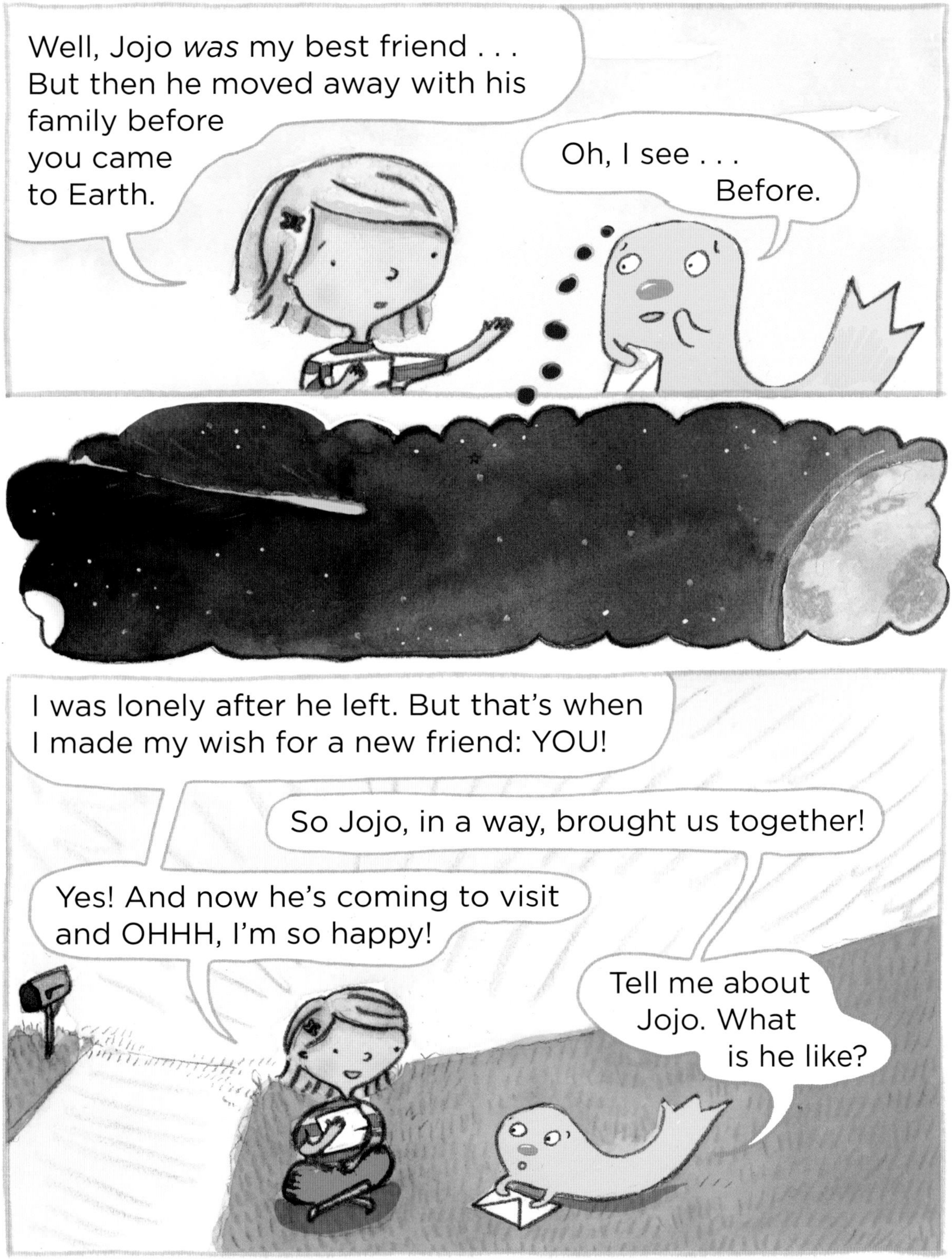
Well, Jojo *was* my best friend . . . But then he moved away with his family before you came to Earth.
Oh, I see . . . Before.
I was lonely after he left. But that's when I made my wish for a new friend: YOU!
So Jojo, in a way, brought us together!
Yes! And now he's coming to visit and OHHH, I'm so happy!
Tell me about Jojo. What is he like?

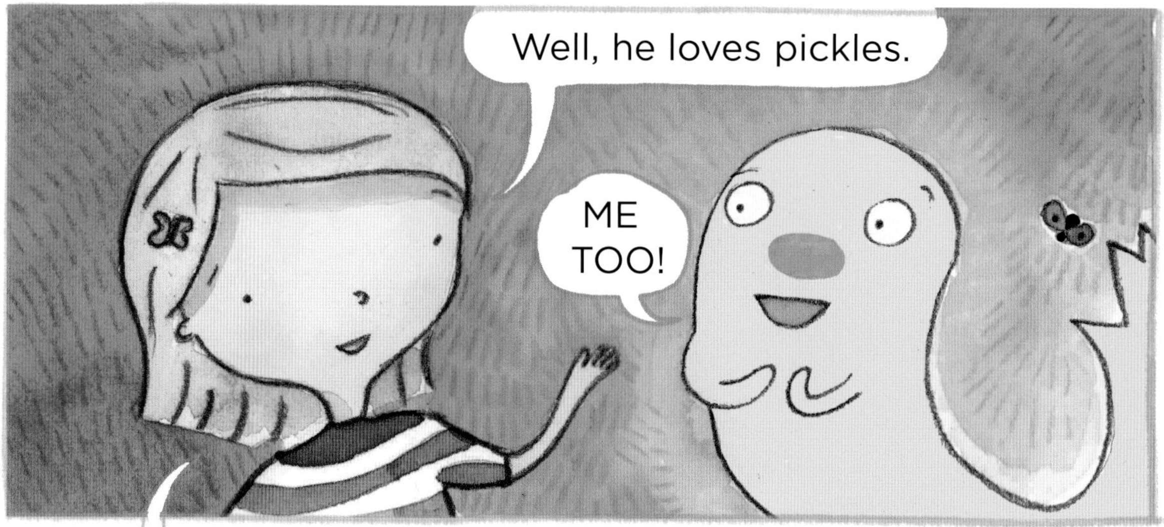
Well, he loves pickles.
ME TOO!

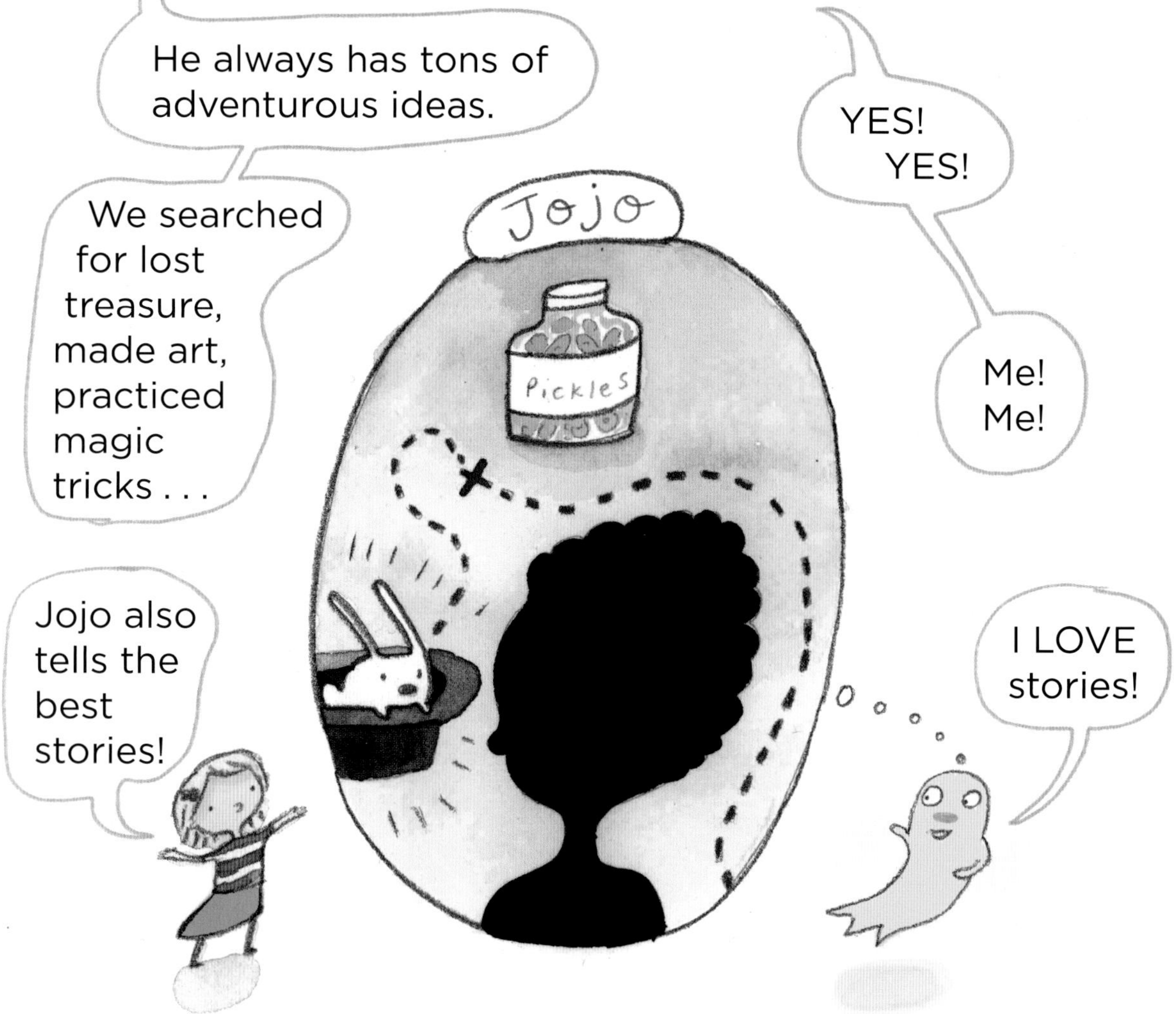
He always has tons of adventurous ideas.
YES! YES!
Jojo
We searched for lost treasure, made art, practiced magic tricks . . .
Pickles
Me! Me!
Jojo also tells the best stories!
I LOVE stories!

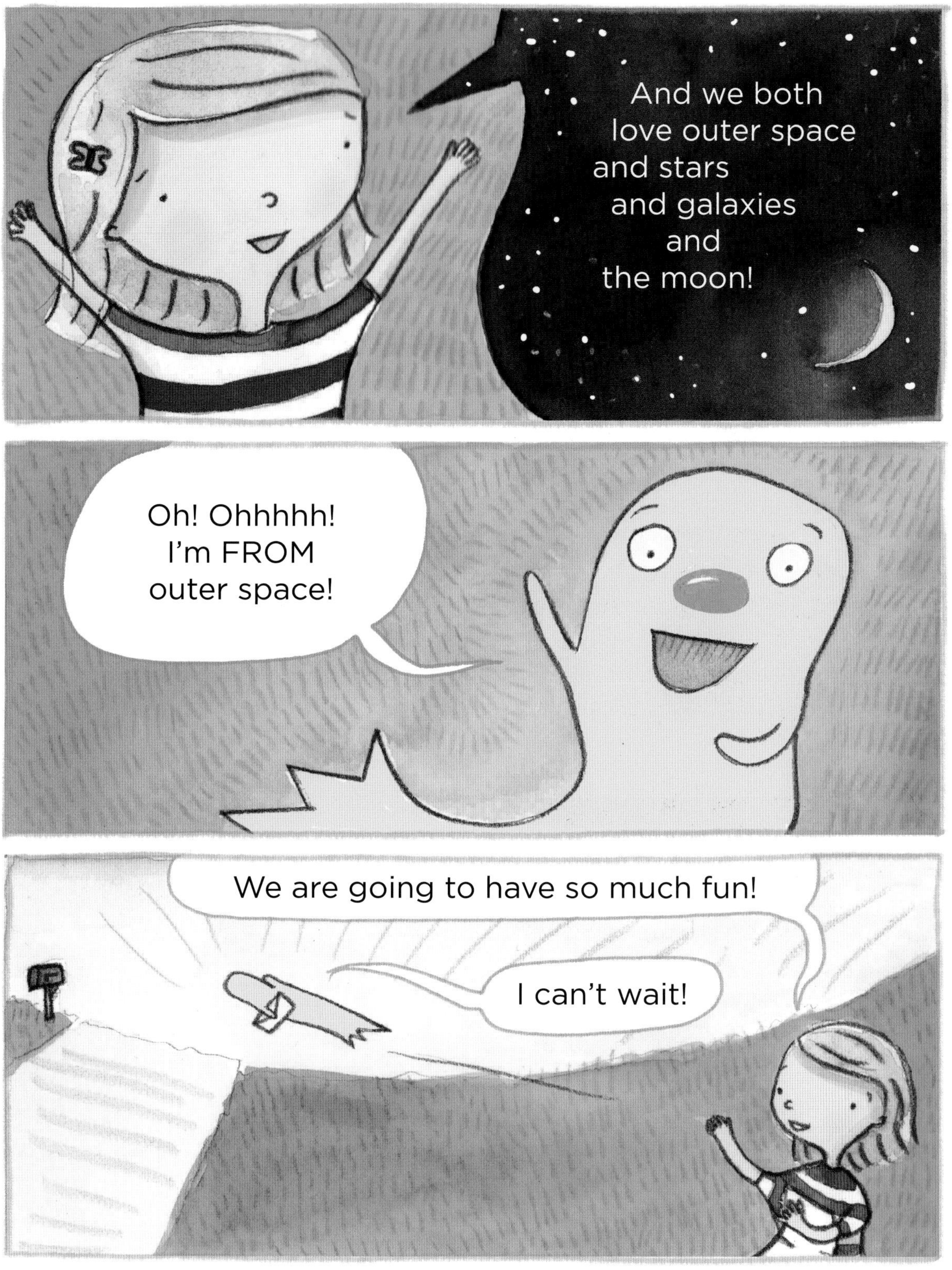
And we both love outer space and stars and galaxies and the moon!
Oh! Ohhhhh! I'm FROM outer space!
We are going to have so much fun!
I can't wait!

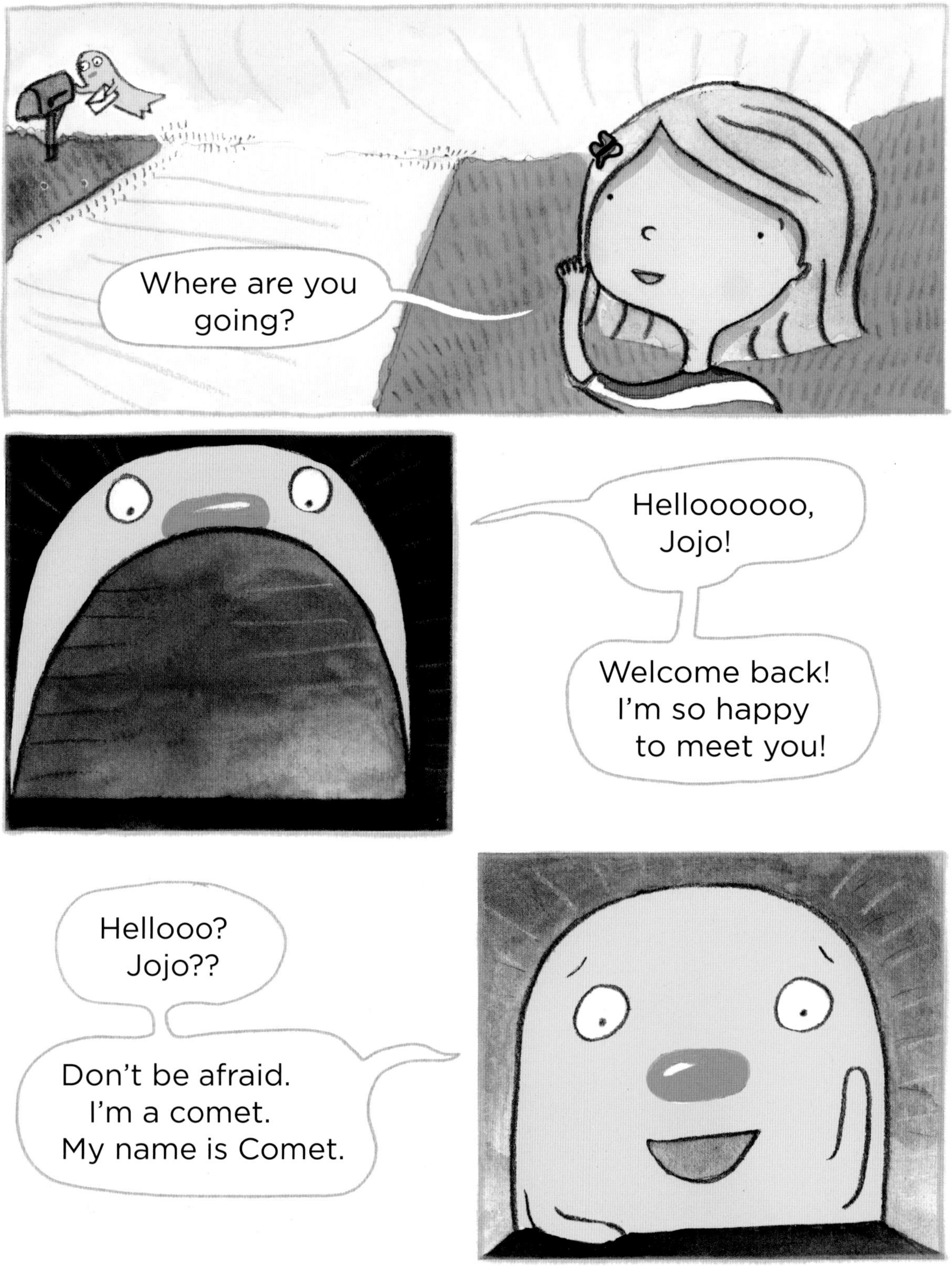
Where are you going?
Hellooooo, Jojo!
Welcome back! I'm so happy to meet you!
Hellooo? Jojo??
Don't be afraid. I'm a comet. My name is Comet.

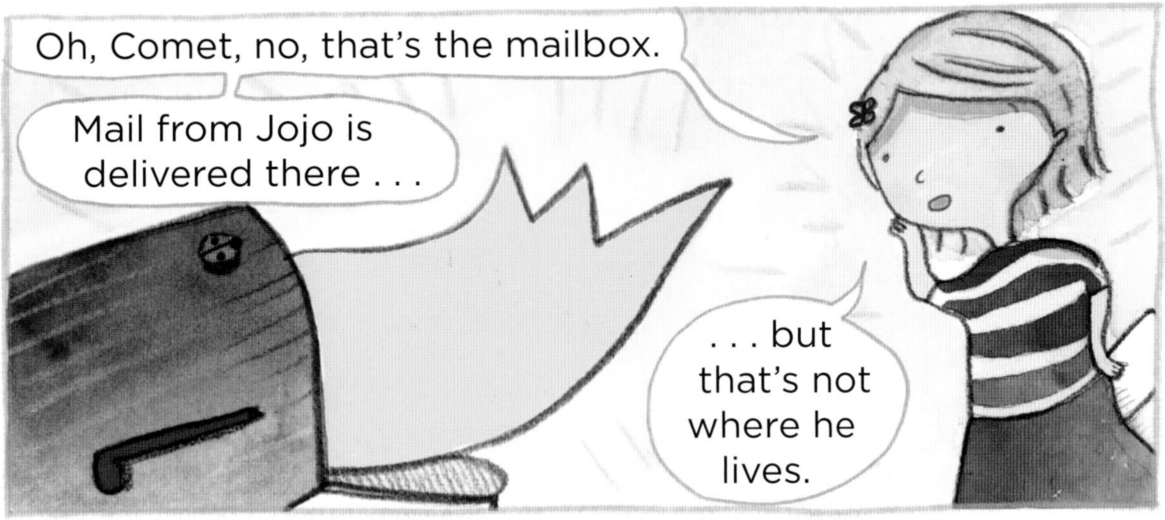
Oh, Comet, no, that's the mailbox.
Mail from Jojo is delivered there . . .
. . . but that's not where he lives.

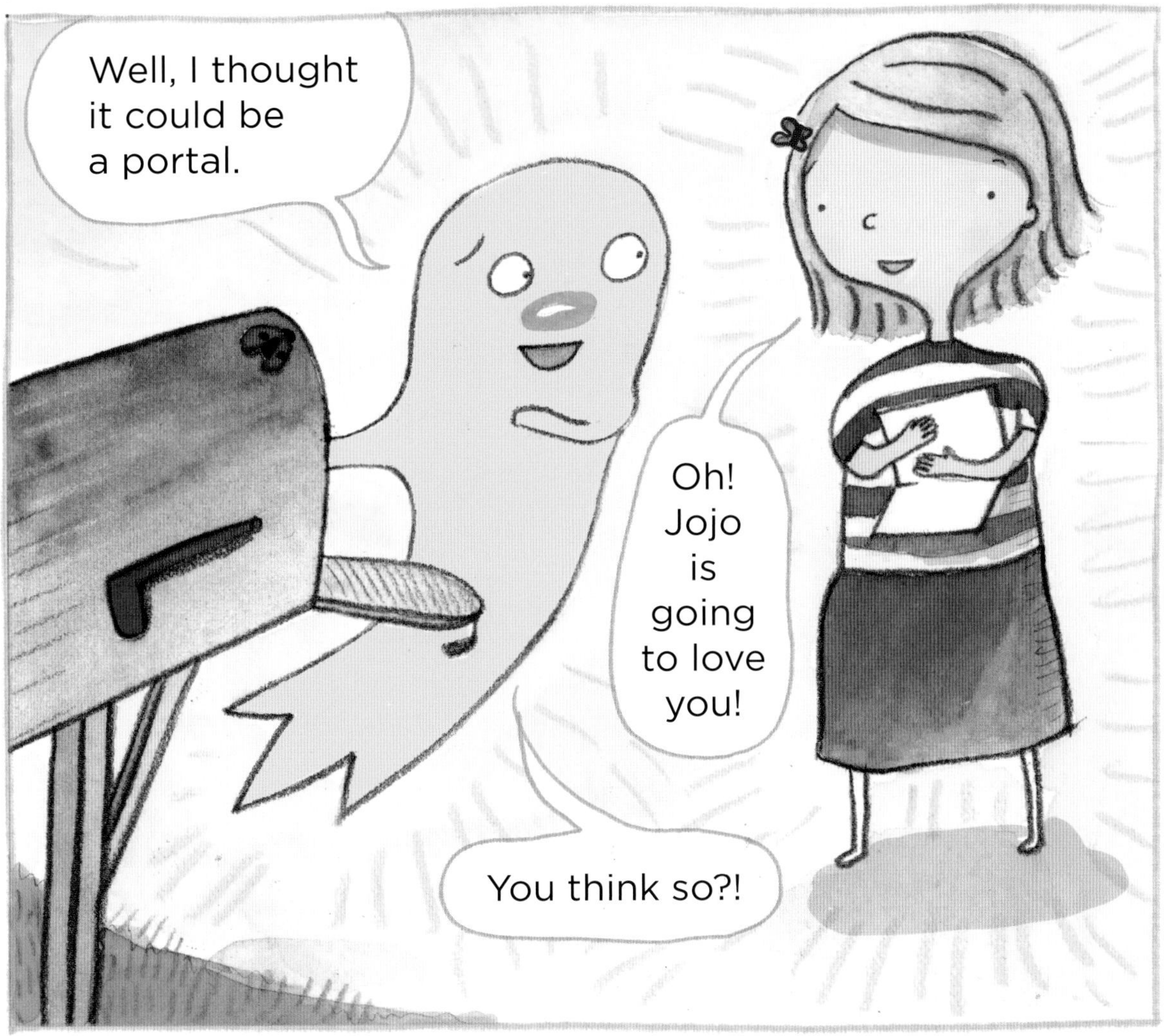
Well, I thought it could be a portal.
Oh! Jojo is going to love you!
You think so?!

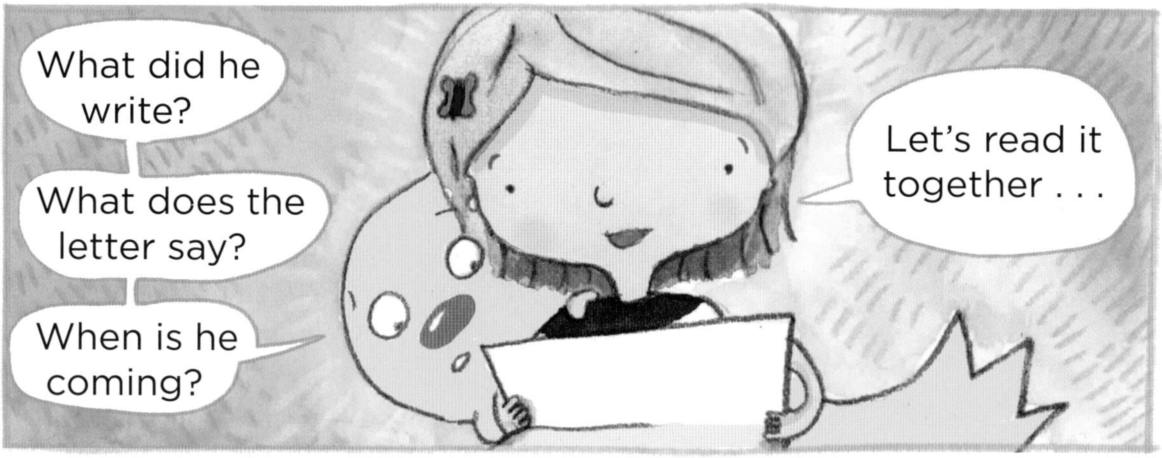
What did he write?
What does the letter say?
When is he coming?
Let's read it together . . .

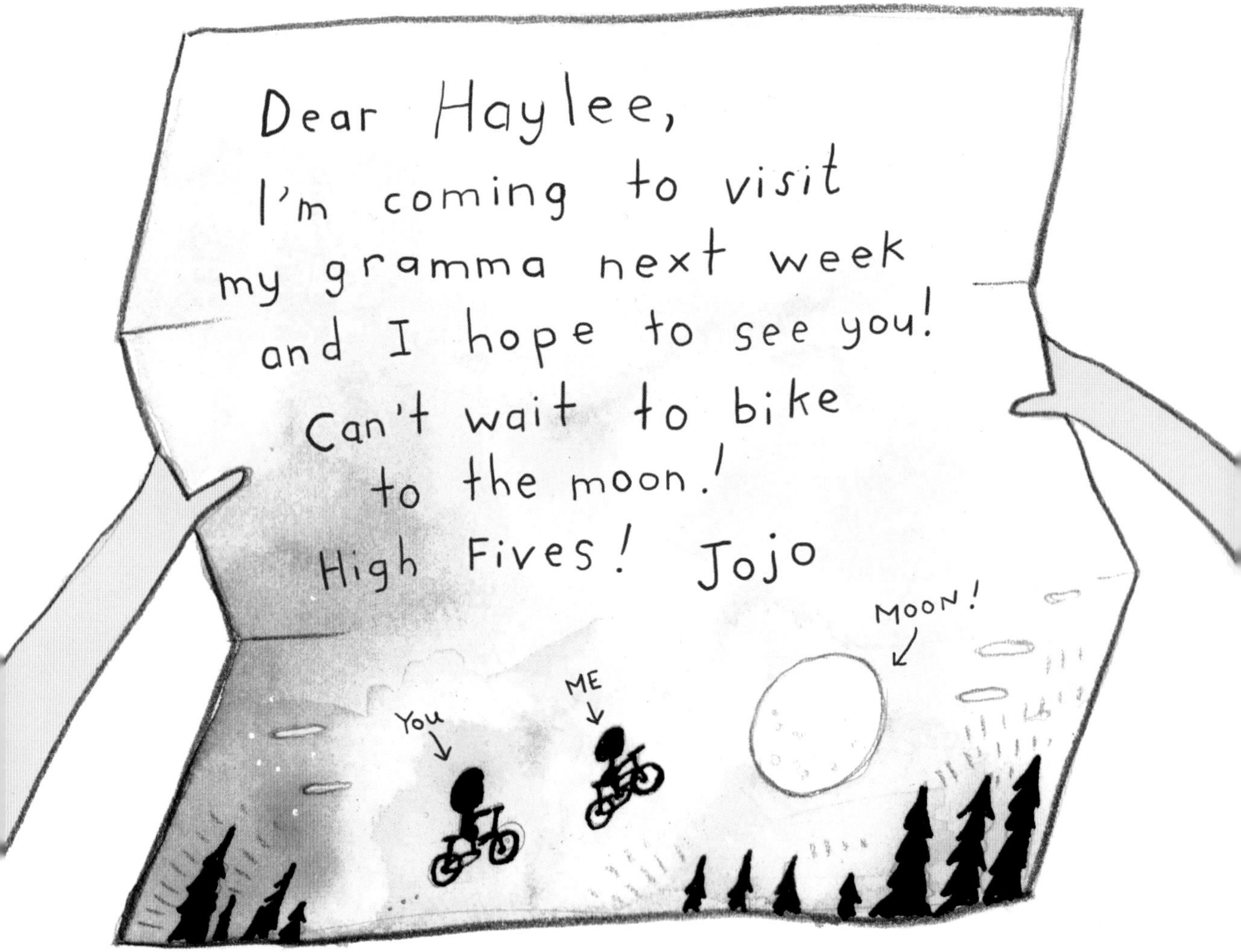
Dear Haylee,
I'm coming to visit my gramma next week and I hope to see you!
Can't wait to bike to the moon!
High Fives! Jojo
MOON!
ME
YOU

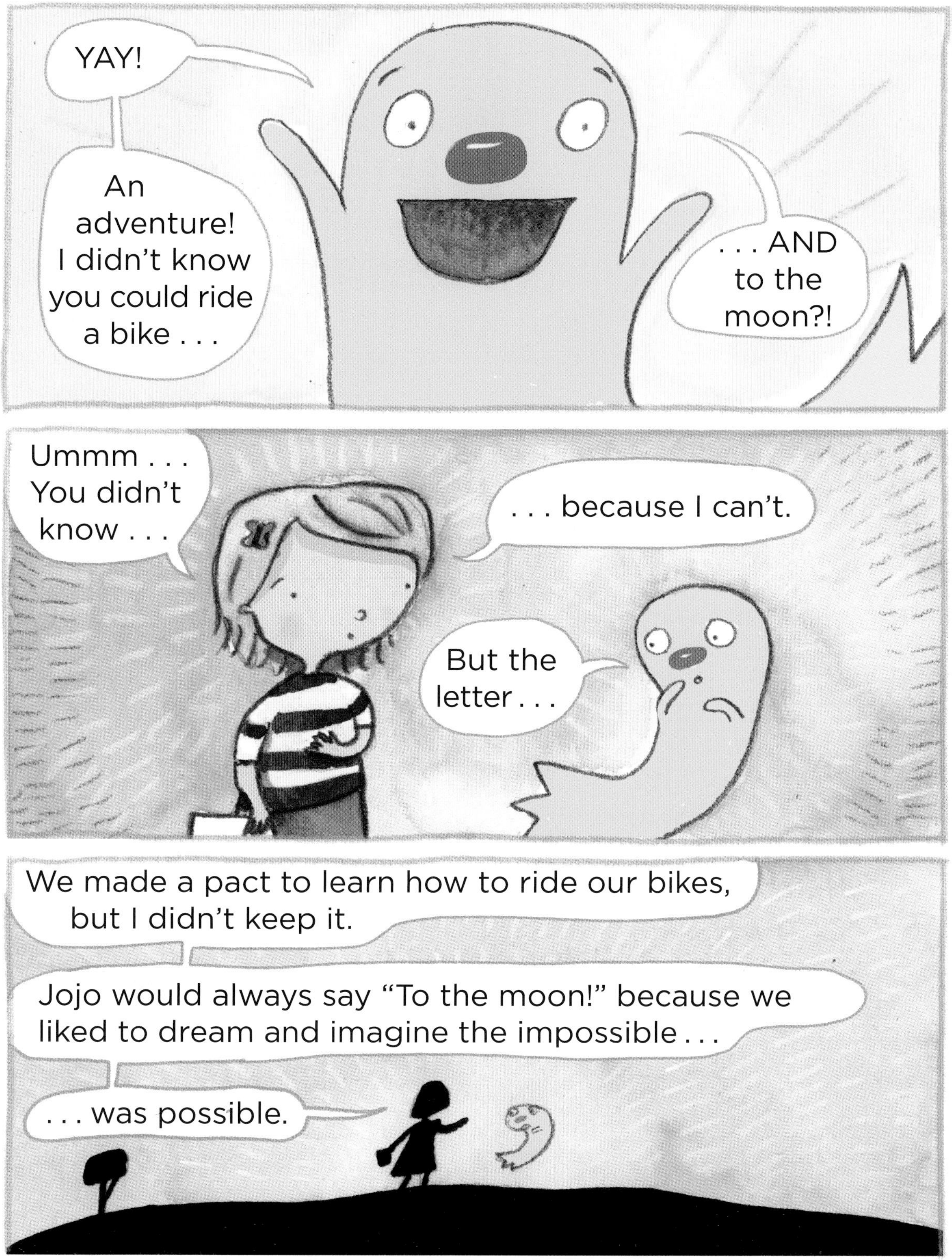
YAY!
An adventure! I didn't know you could ride a bike . . .
. . . AND to the moon?!
Ummm . . . You didn't know . . .
. . . because I can't.
But the letter . . .
We made a pact to learn how to ride our bikes, but I didn't keep it.
Jojo would always say "To the moon!" because we liked to dream and imagine the impossible . . .
. . . was possible.

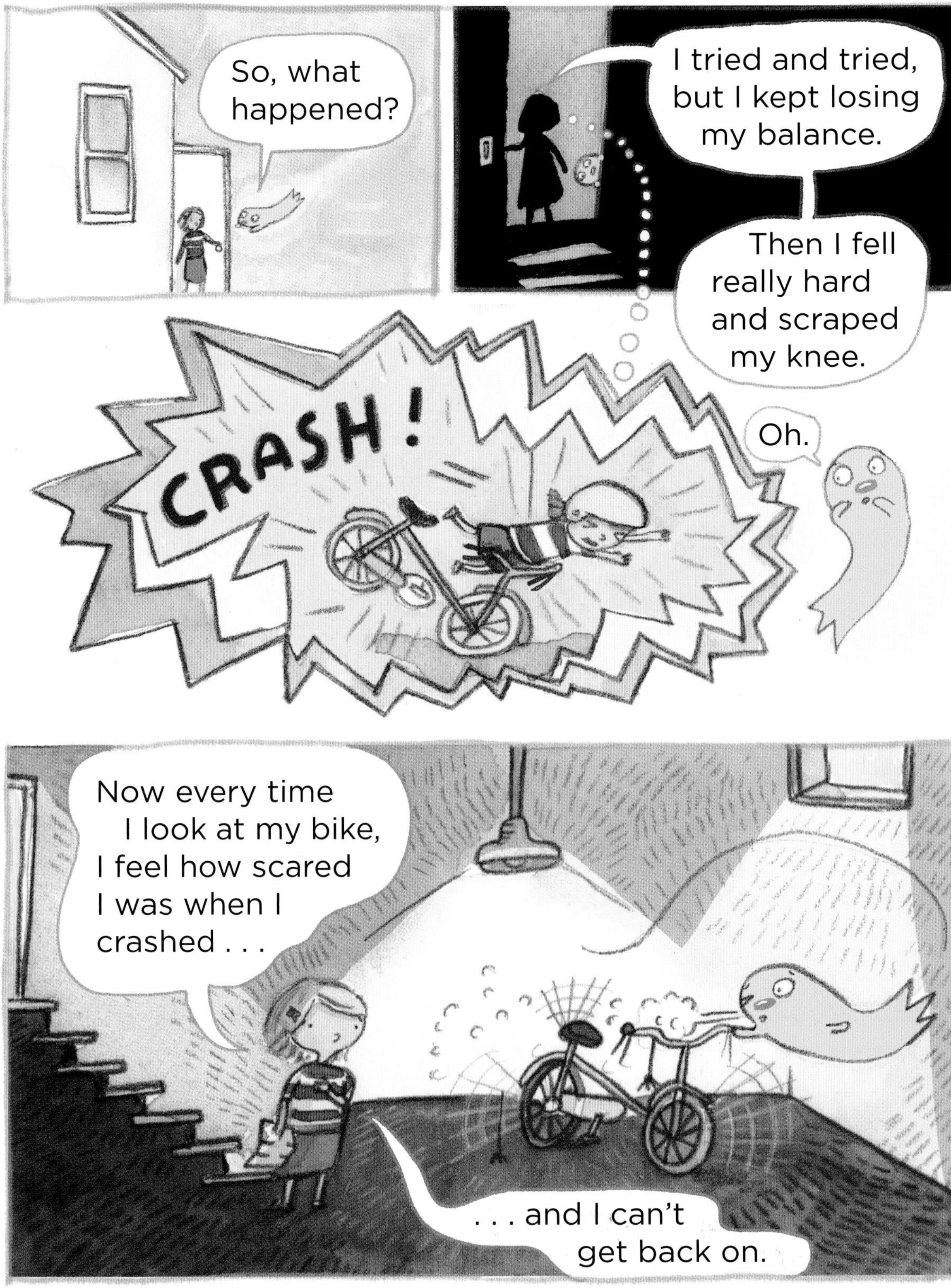
So, what happened?
I tried and tried, but I kept losing my balance.
Then I fell really hard and scraped my knee.
CRASH!
Oh.
Now every time I look at my bike, I feel how scared I was when I crashed . . .
. . . and I can't get back on.

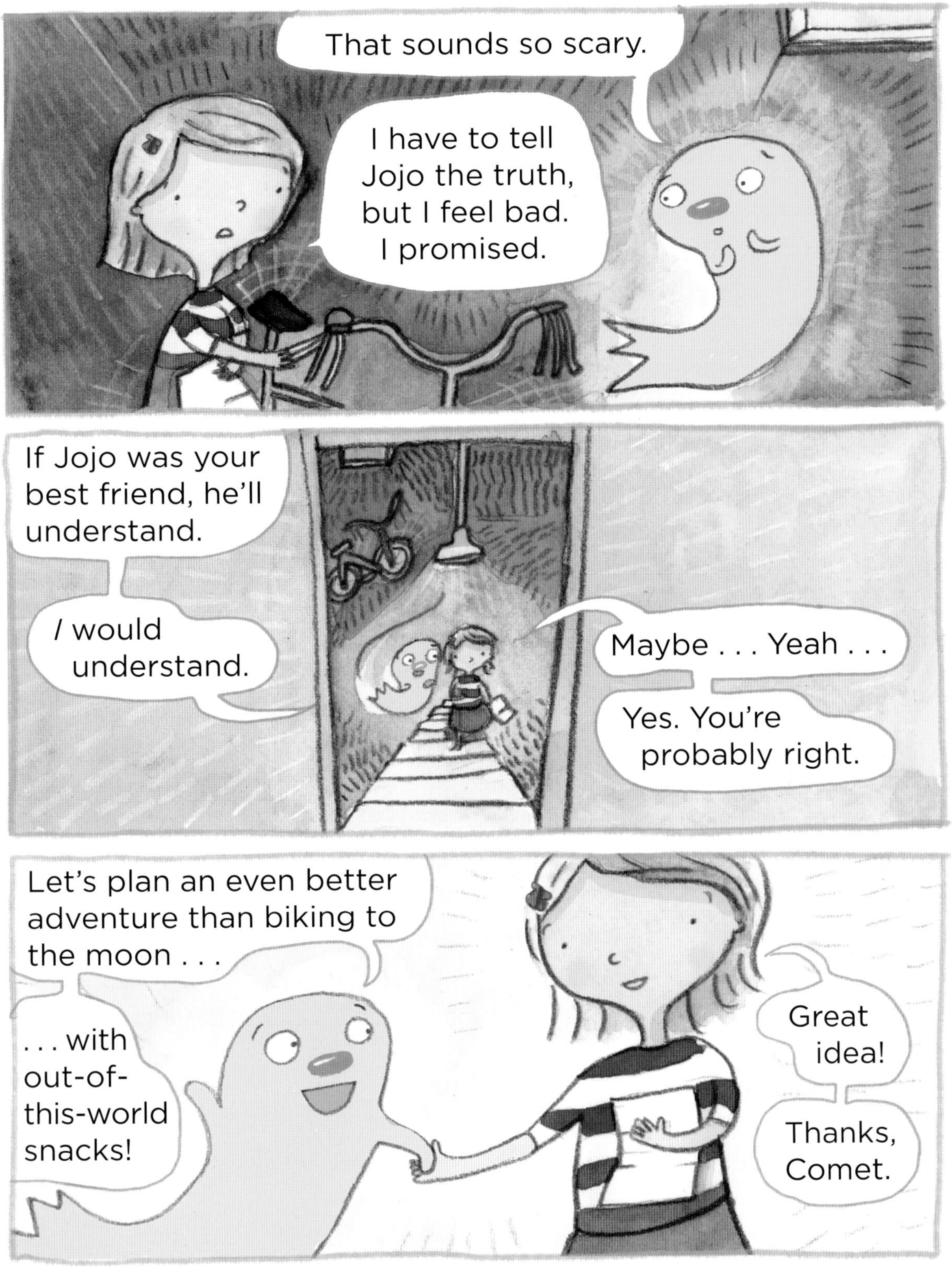
That sounds so scary.
I have to tell Jojo the truth, but I feel bad. I promised.
If Jojo was your best friend, he'll understand.
I would understand.
Maybe . . . Yeah . . .
Yes. You're probably right.
Let's plan an even better adventure than biking to the moon . . .
. . . with out-of-this-world snacks!
Great idea!
Thanks, Comet.

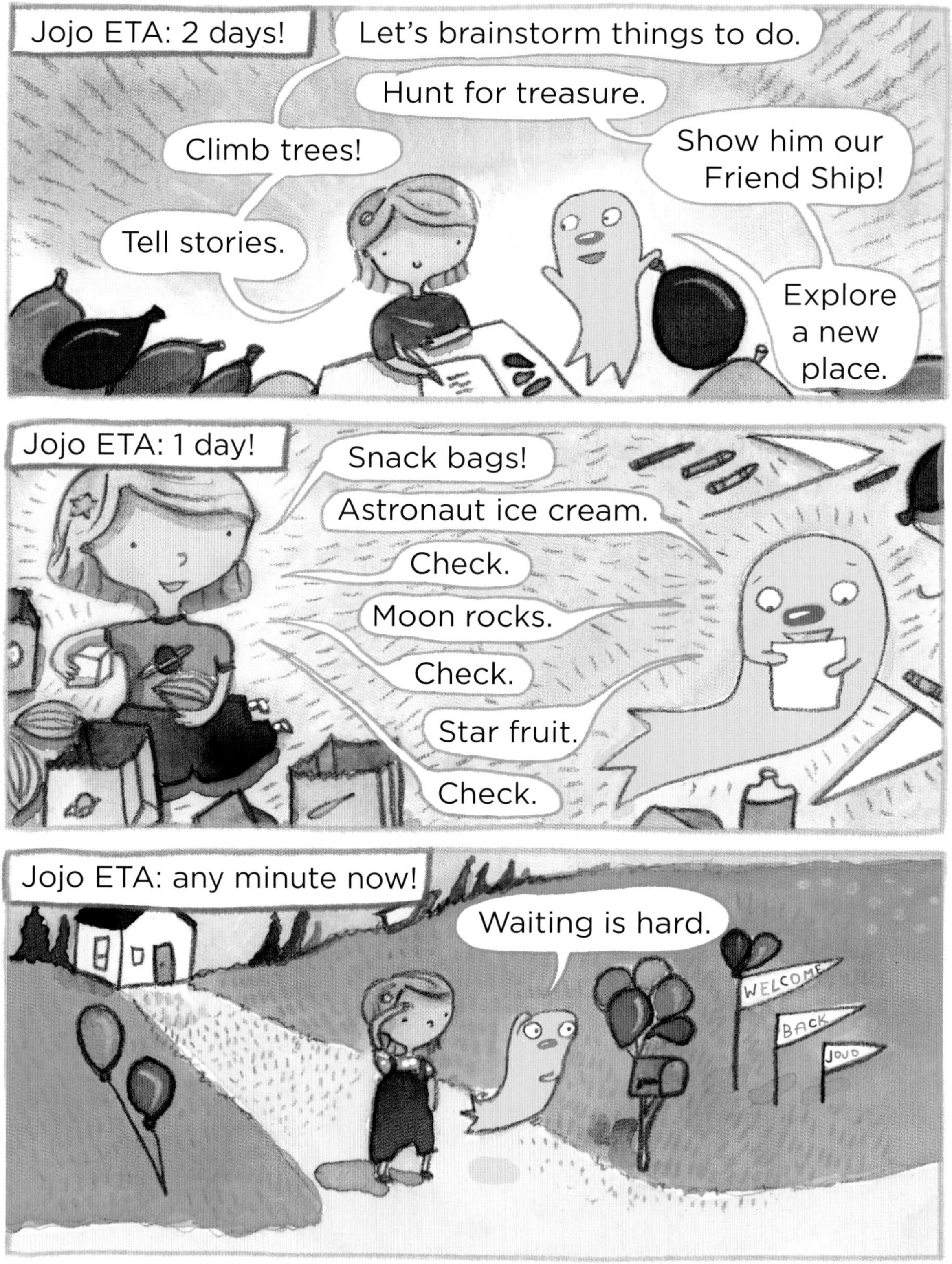
Jojo ETA: 2 days!
Let's brainstorm things to do.
Hunt for treasure.
Climb trees!
Show him our Friend Ship!
Tell stories.
Explore a new place.
Jojo ETA: 1 day!
Snack bags!
Astronaut ice cream.
Check.
Moon rocks.
Check.
Star fruit.
Check.
Jojo ETA: any minute now!
Waiting is hard.
WELCOME
BACK
JOJO

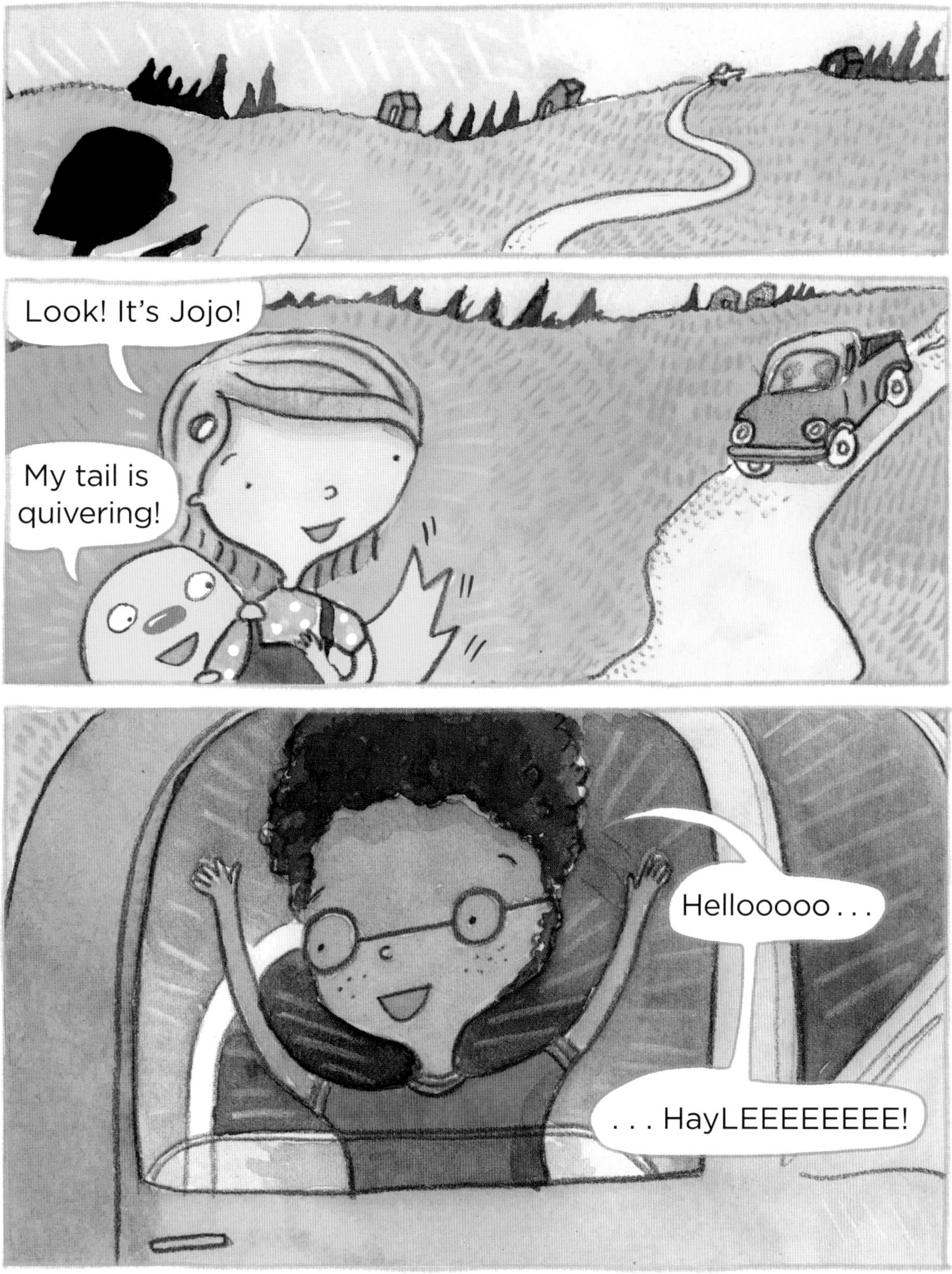
Look! It's Jojo!
My tail is quivering!
Hellooooo . . .
. . . HayLEEEEEEEE!

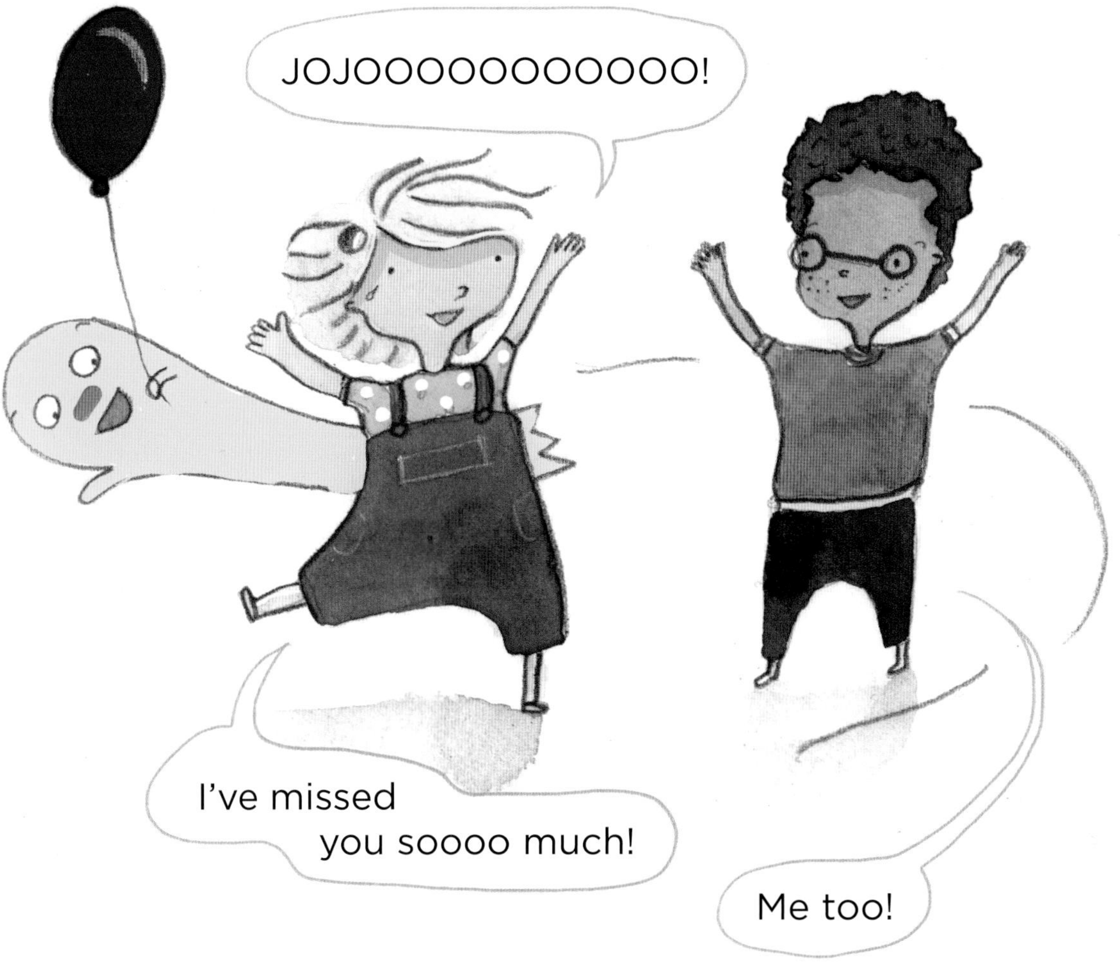
JOJOOOOOOOOOOOO!
I've missed you soooo much!
Me too!

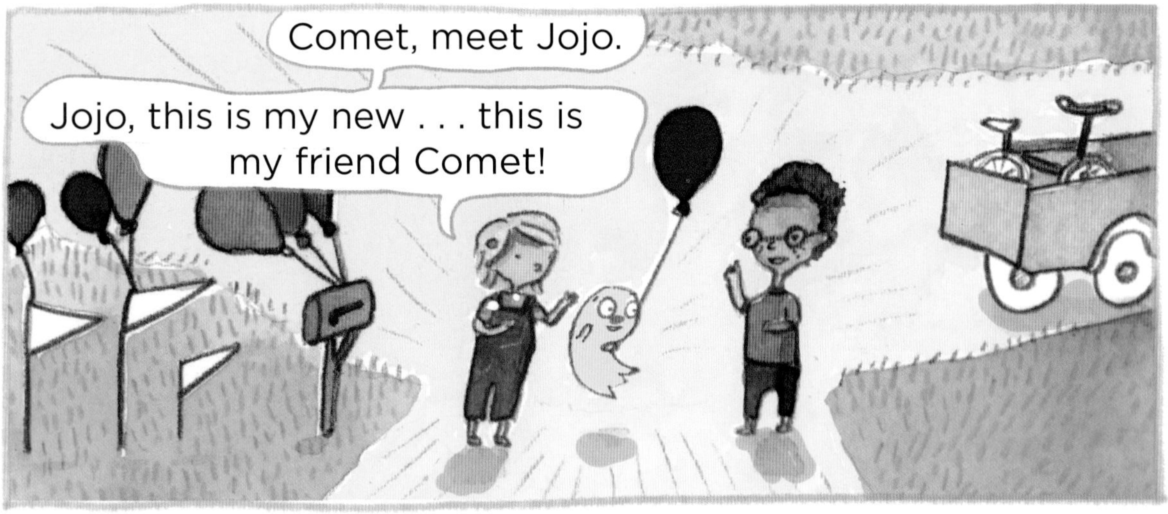
Comet, meet Jojo.
Jojo, this is my new . . . this is my friend Comet!

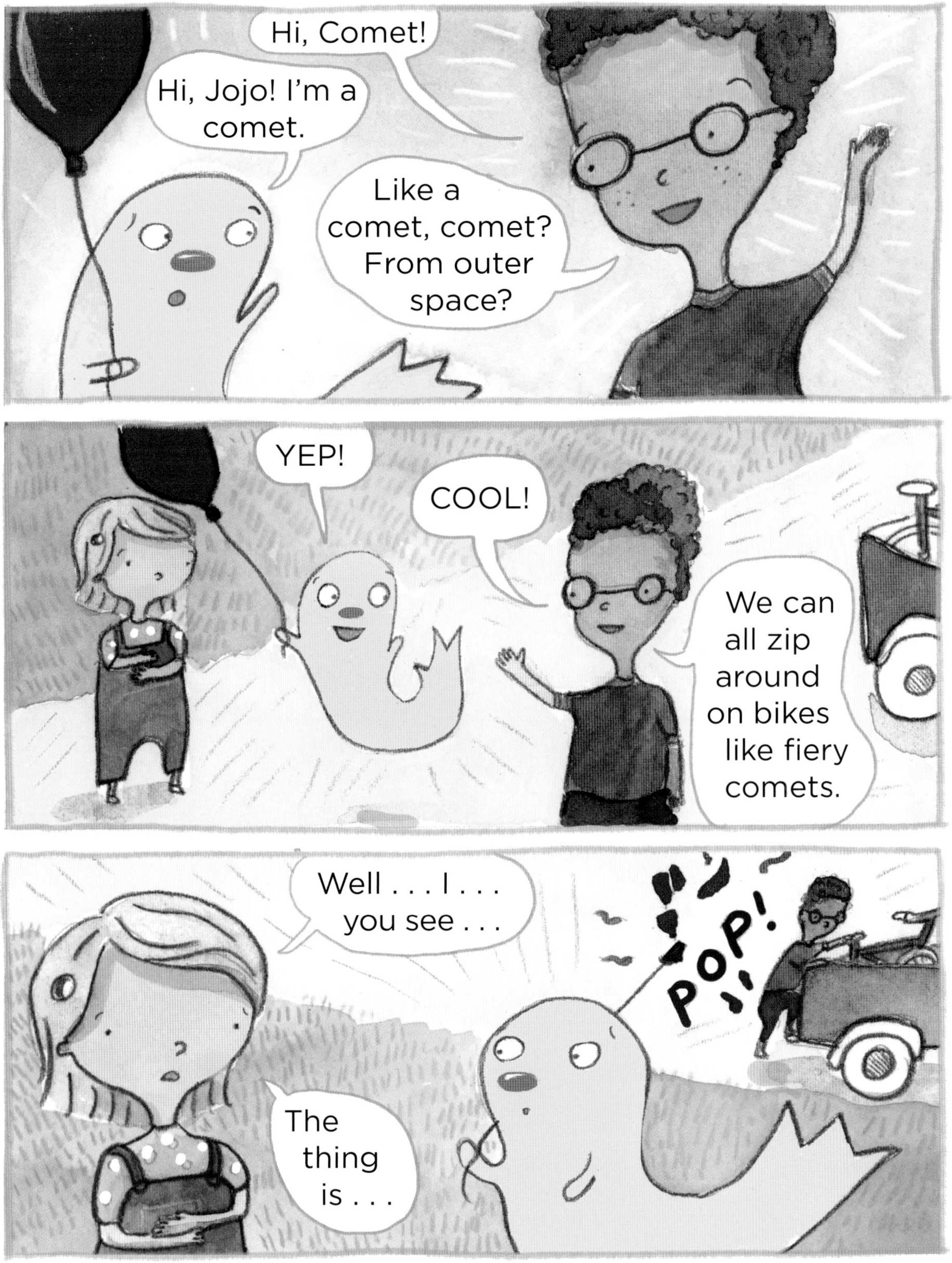
Hi, Comet!
Hi, Jojo! I'm a comet.
Like a comet, comet? From outer space?
YEP!
COOL!
We can all zip around on bikes like fiery comets.
Well . . . I . . . you see . . .
POP!
The thing is . . .

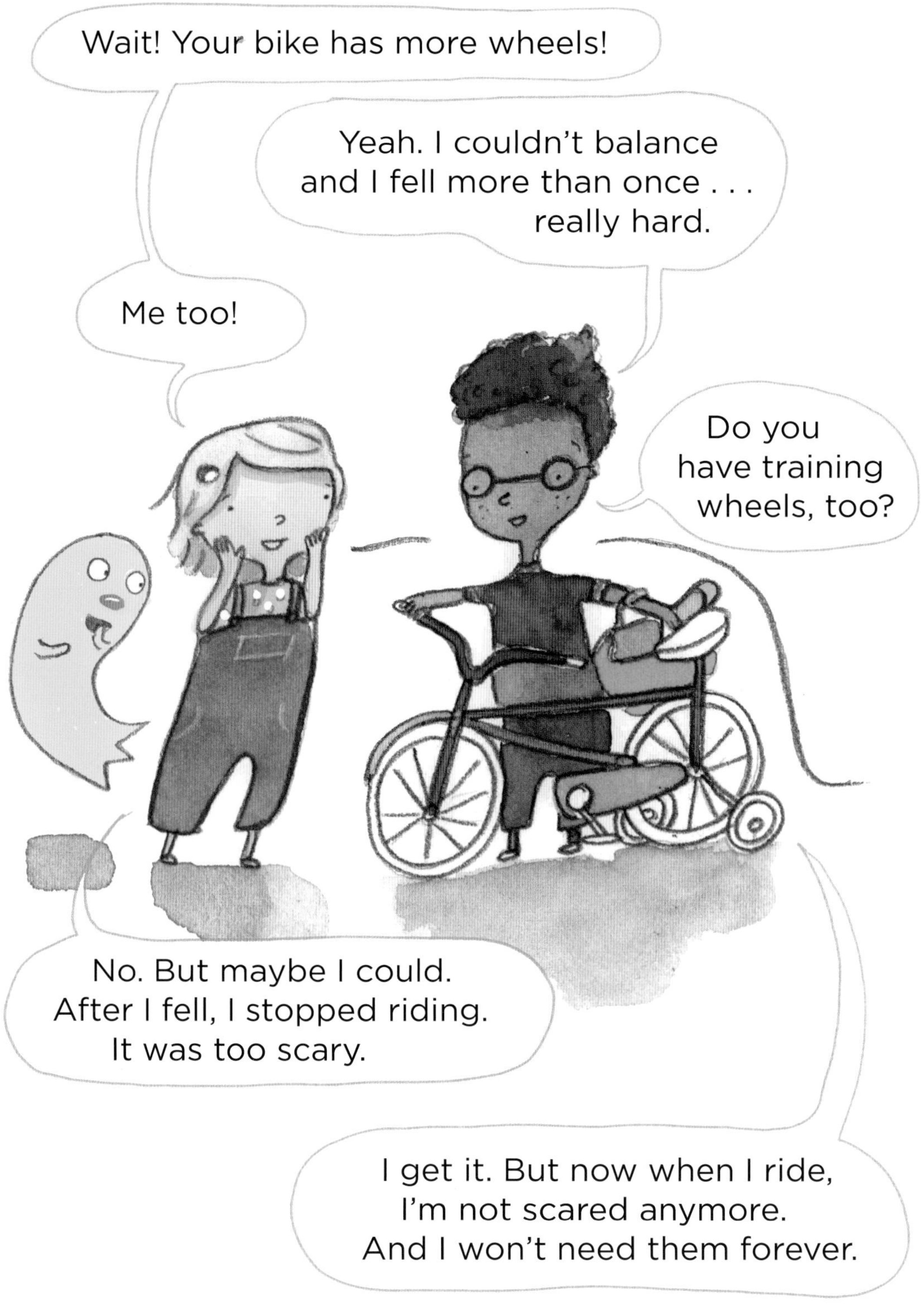
Wait! Your bike has more wheels!
Yeah. I couldn't balance and I fell more than once . . . really hard.
Me too!
Do you have training wheels, too?
No. But maybe I could. After I fell, I stopped riding. It was too scary.
I get it. But now when I ride, I'm not scared anymore. And I won't need them forever.

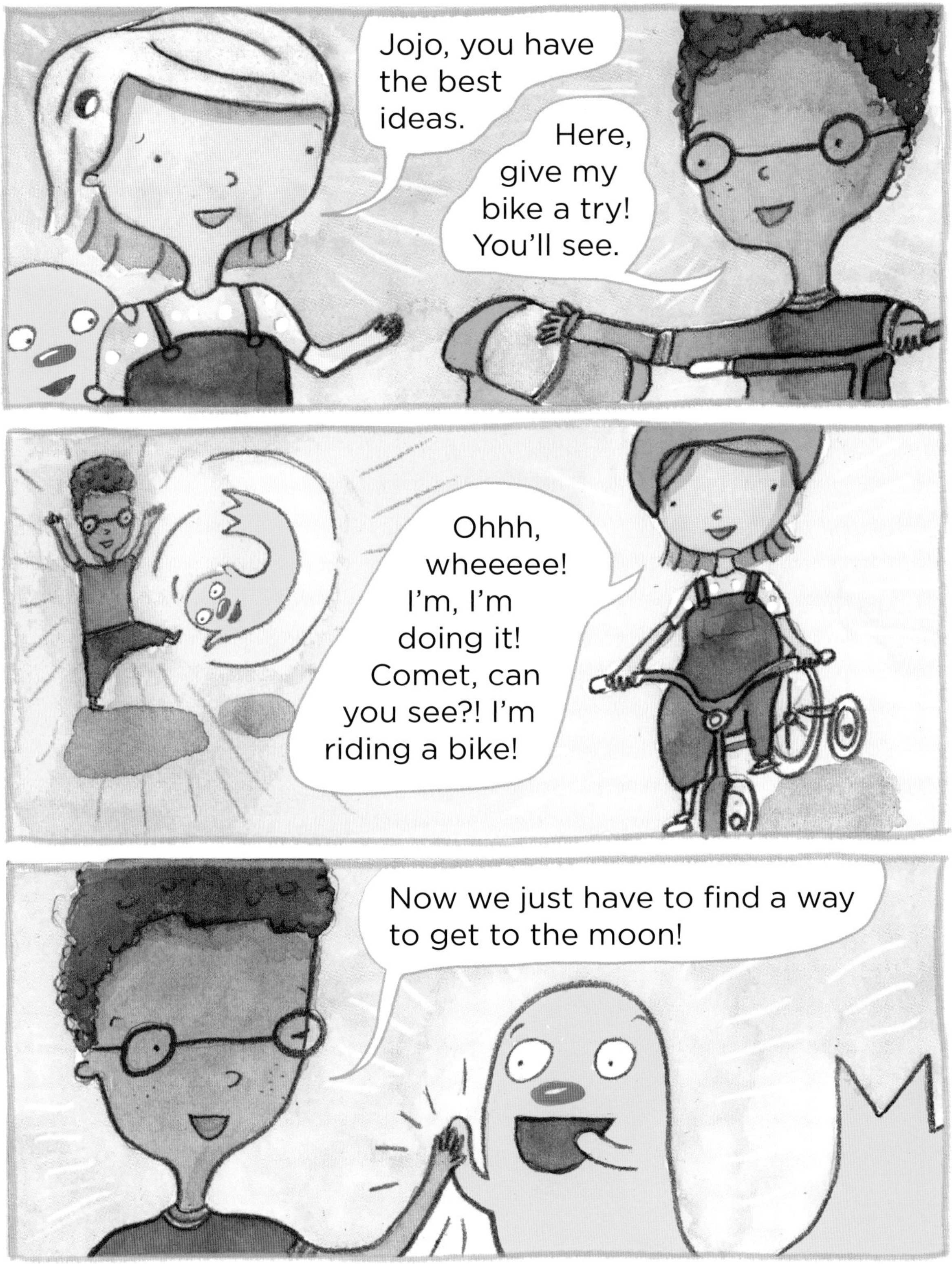
Jojo, you have the best ideas.
Here, give my bike a try! You'll see.
Ohhh, wheeeee! I'm, I'm doing it! Comet, can you see?! I'm riding a bike!
Now we just have to find a way to get to the moon!

# Comet Goes for Some Test Rides

Unicycle

Tricycle

Recumbent Bike

Bicycle Motocross (BMX)

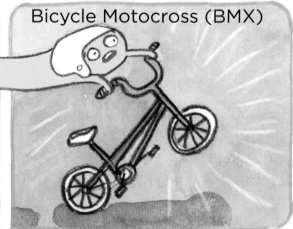

Tandem Bike

2+1

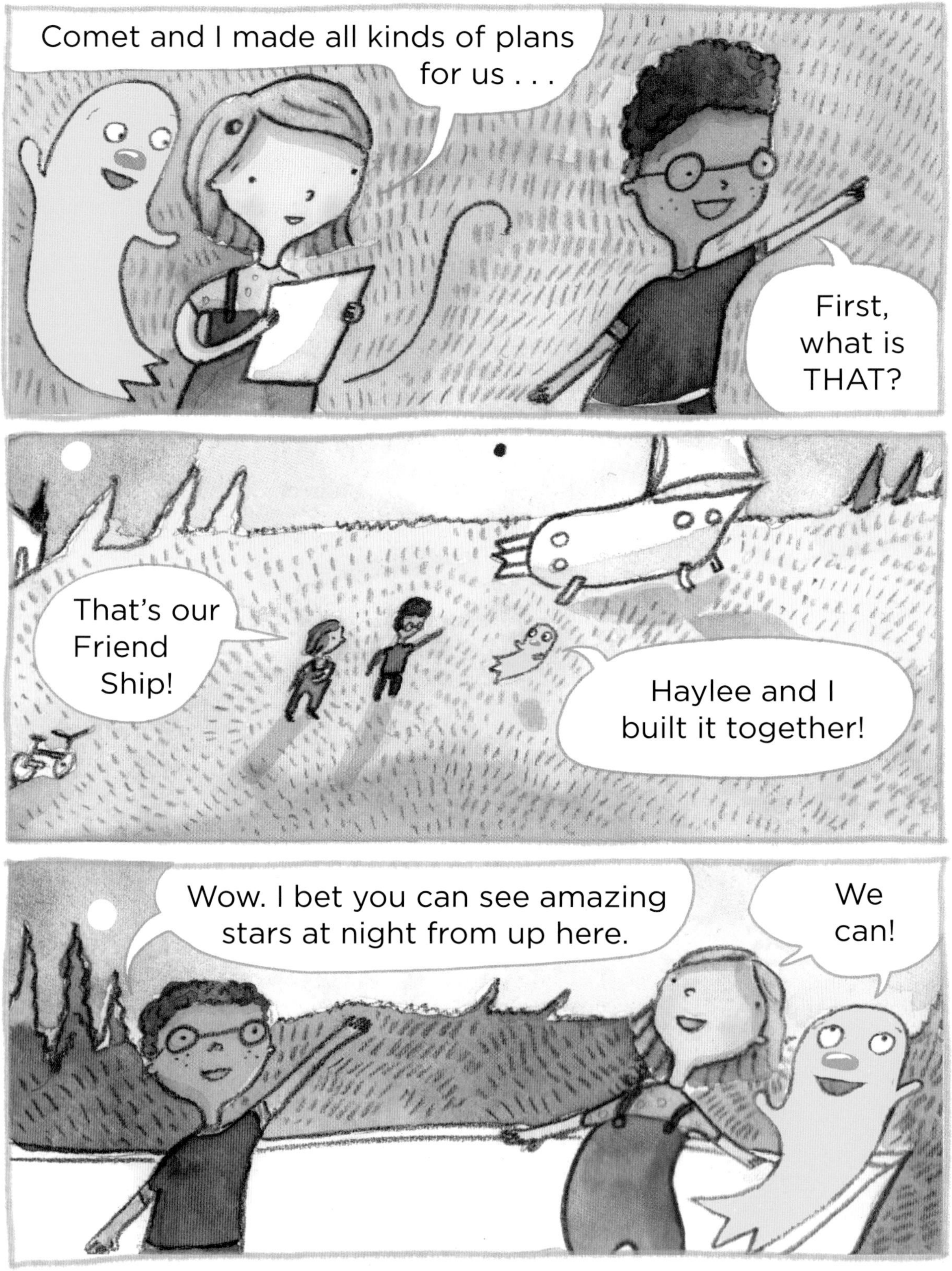
Comet and I made all kinds of plans for us . . .
First, what is THAT?
That's our Friend Ship!
Haylee and I built it together!
Wow. I bet you can see amazing stars at night from up here.
We can!

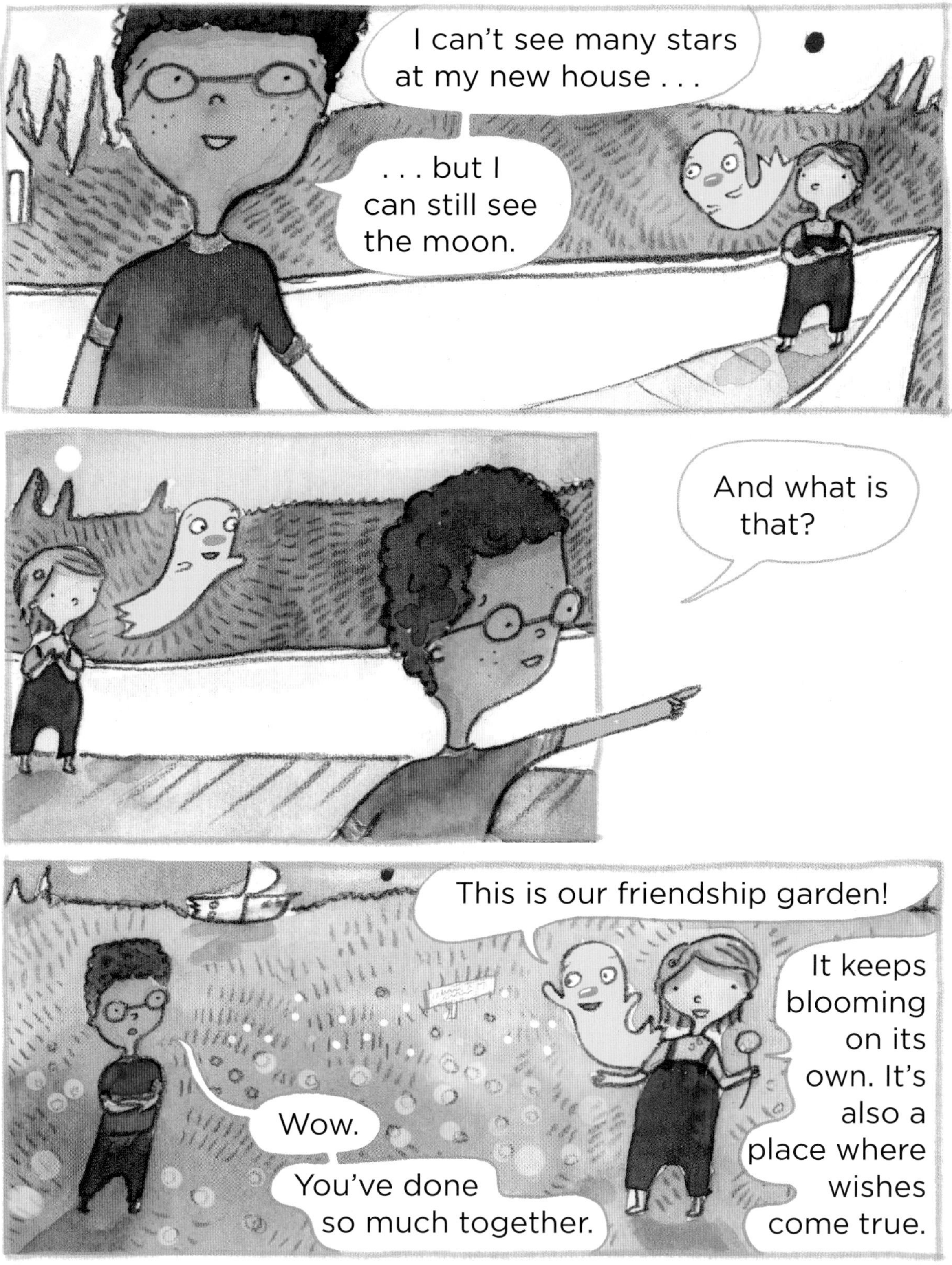

I can't see many stars at my new house . . .
. . . but I can still see the moon.
And what is that?
This is our friendship garden!
It keeps blooming on its own. It's also a place where wishes come true.
Wow.
You've done so much together.

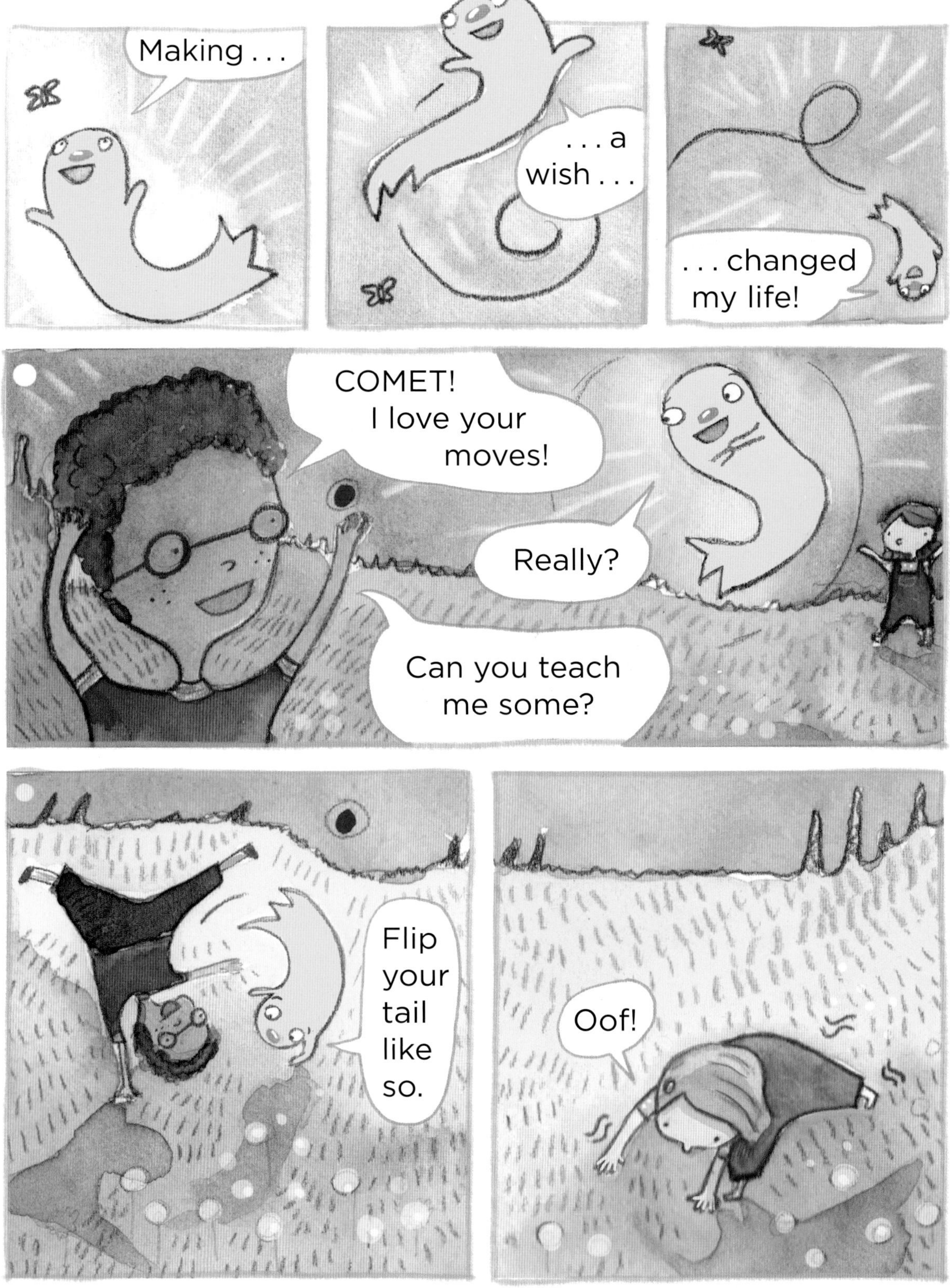
Making . . .
. . . a wish . . .
. . . changed my life!
COMET! I love your moves!
Really?
Can you teach me some?
Flip your tail like so.
Oof!

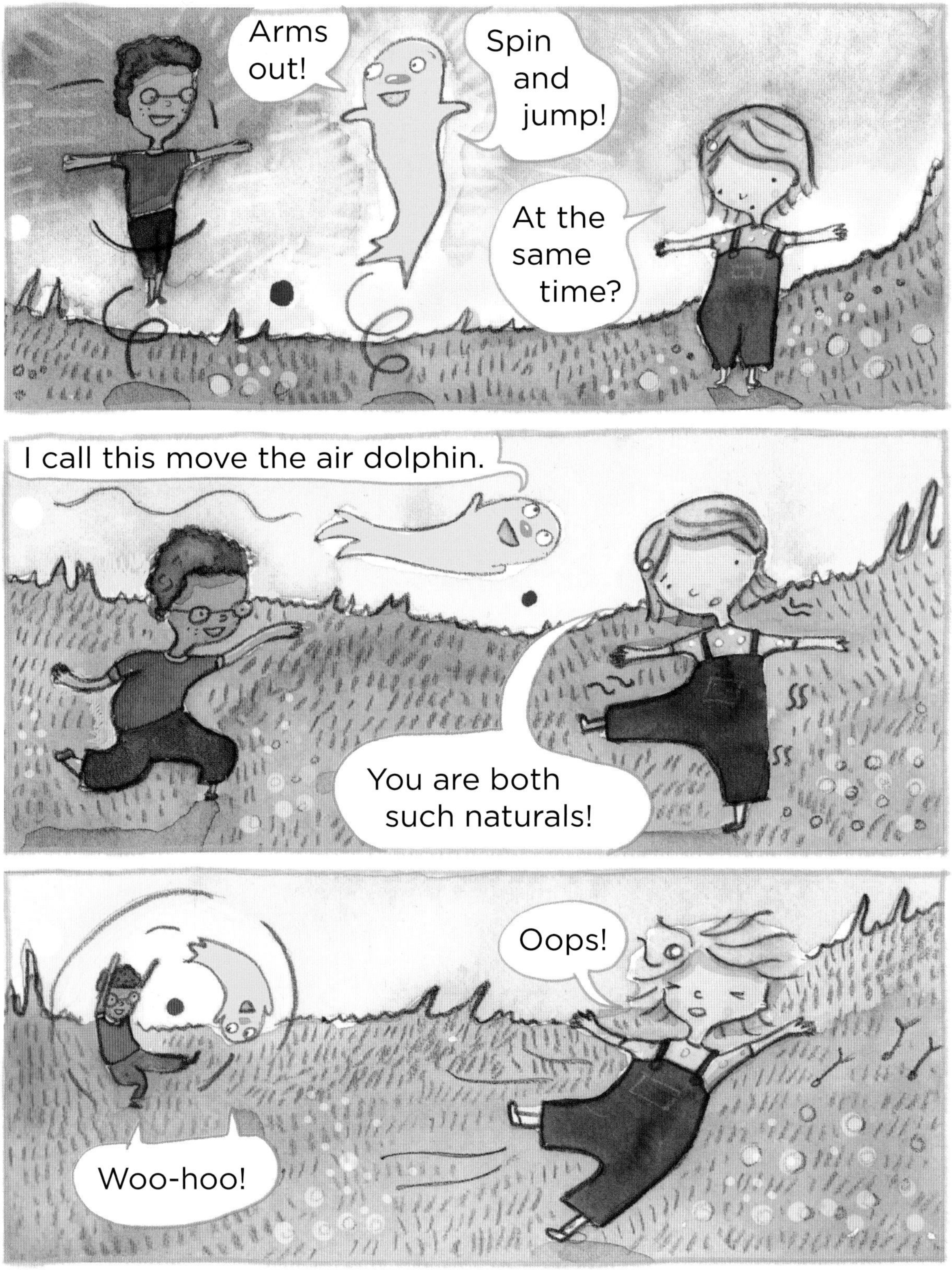
Arms out!
Spin and jump!
At the same time?
I call this move the air dolphin.
You are both such naturals!
Oops!
Woo-hoo!

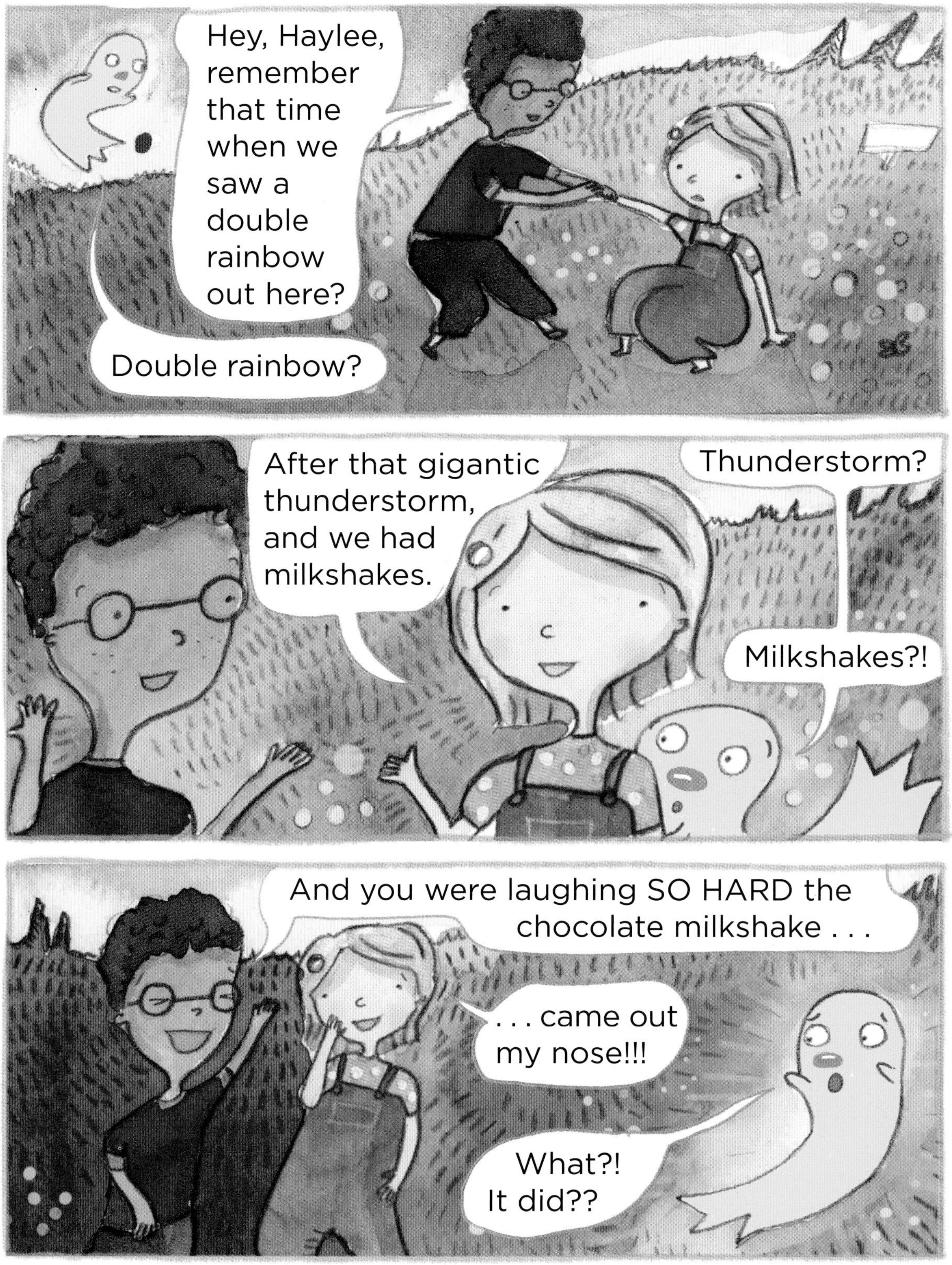
Hey, Haylee, remember that time when we saw a double rainbow out here?
Double rainbow?
After that gigantic thunderstorm, and we had milkshakes.
Thunderstorm?
Milkshakes?!
And you were laughing SO HARD the chocolate milkshake . . .
. . . came out my nose!!!
What?! It did??

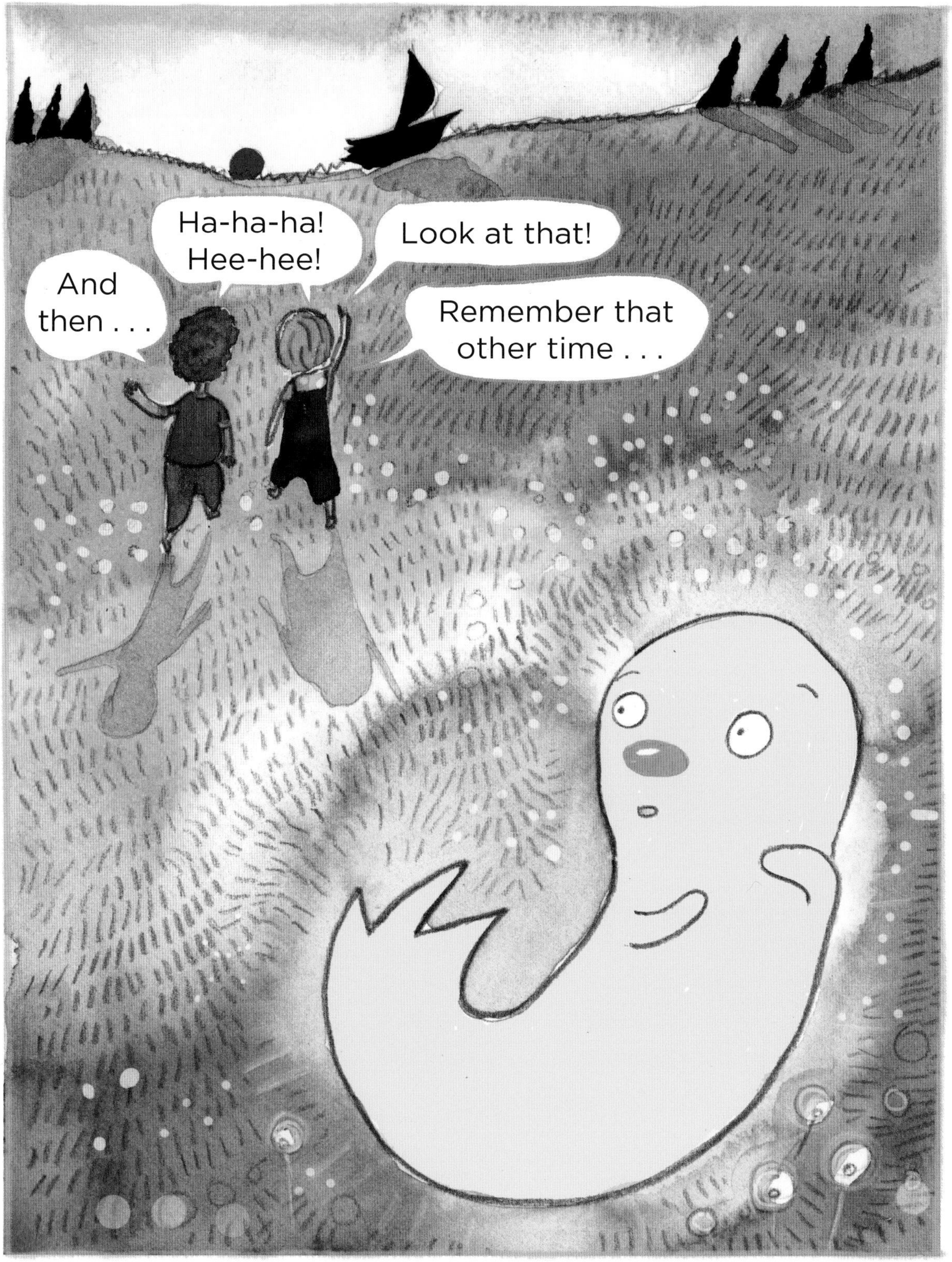
And then . . .
Ha-ha-ha! Hee-hee!
Look at that!
Remember that other time . . .

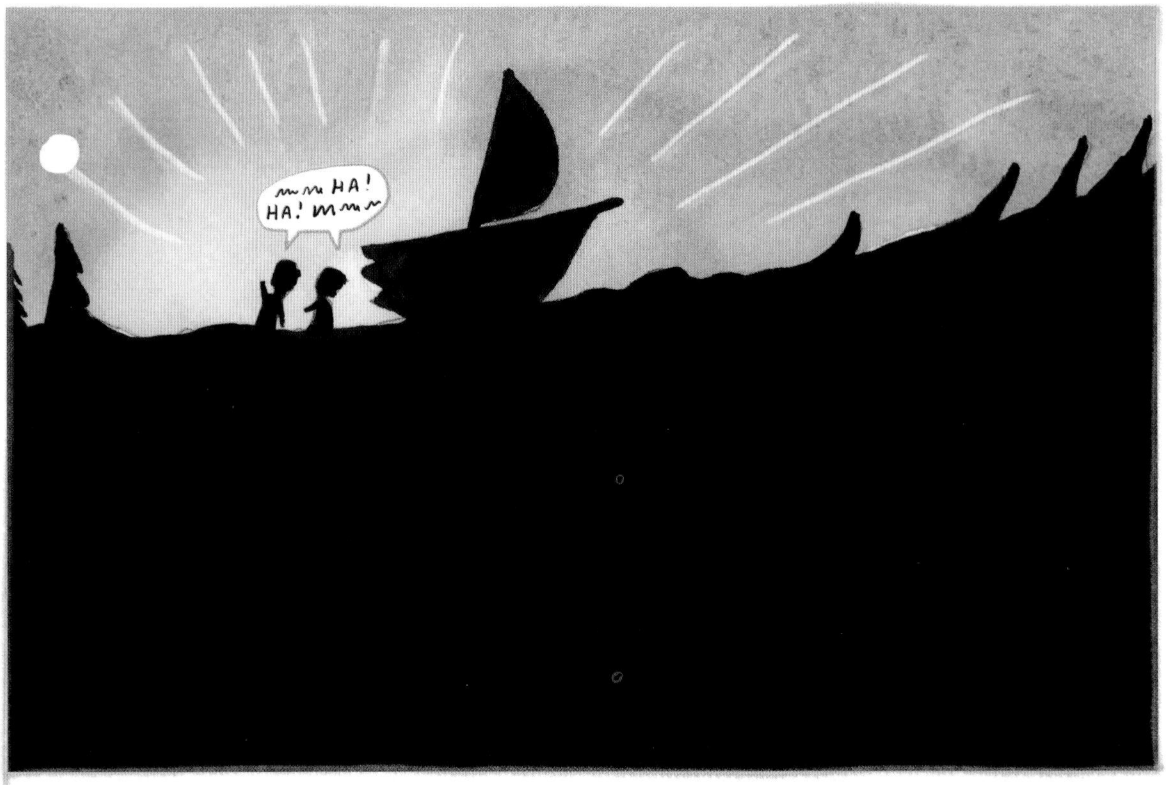
mmm HA! HA! mmm

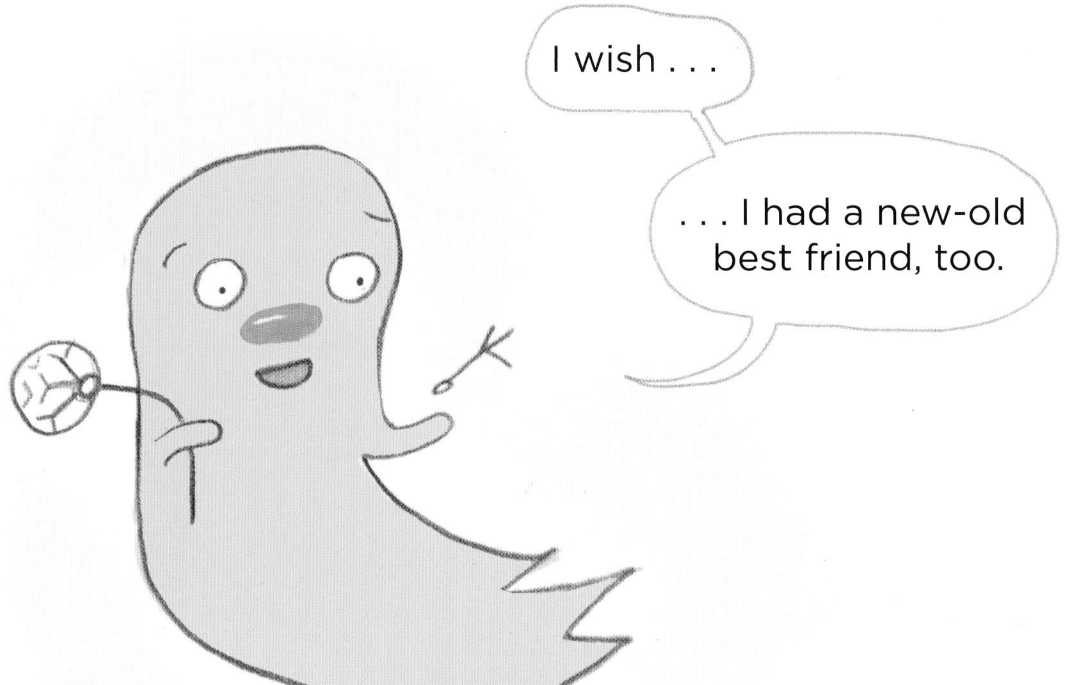
I wish . . .
. . . I had a new-old best friend, too.

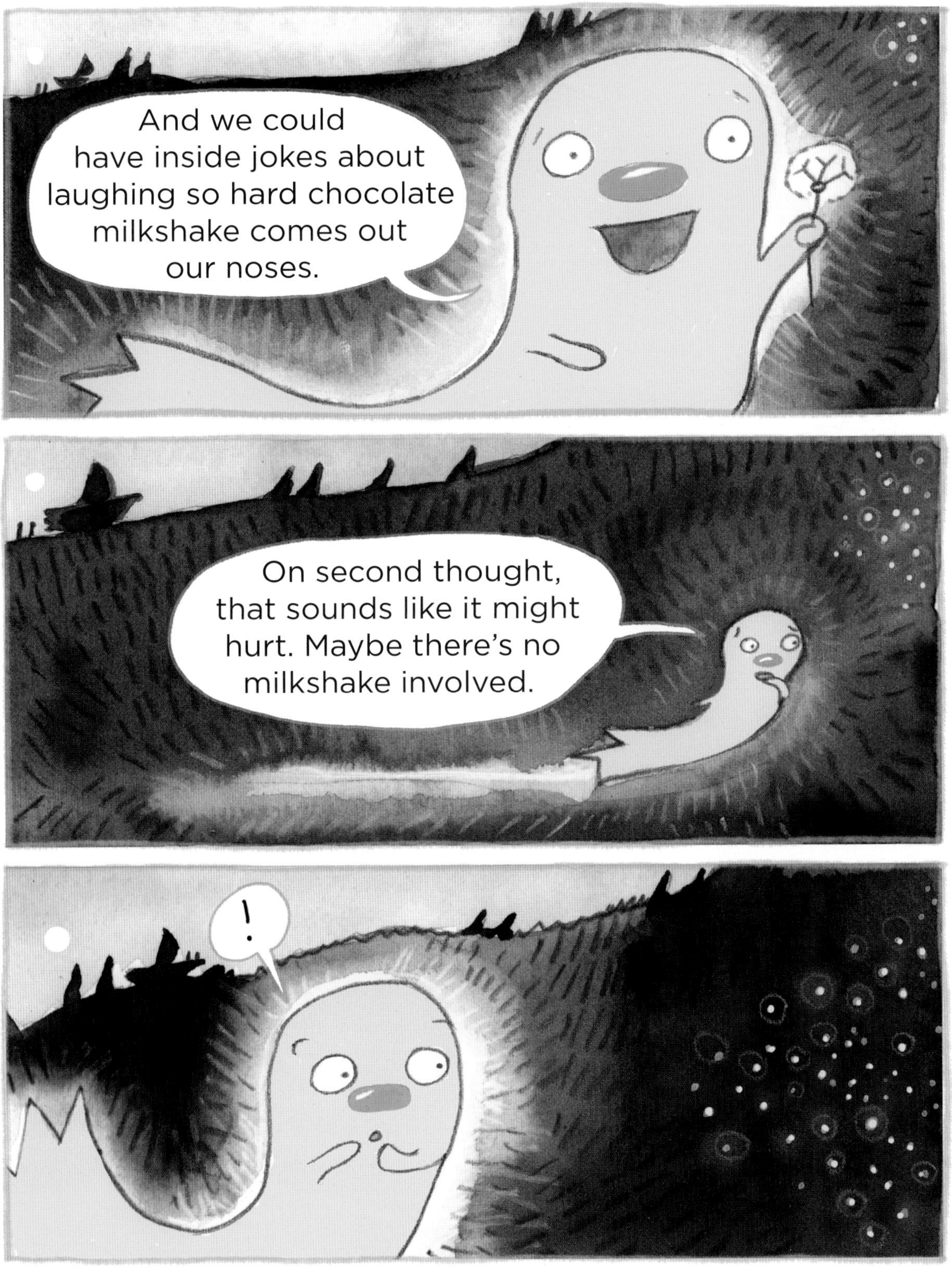
And we could have inside jokes about laughing so hard chocolate milkshake comes out our noses.
On second thought, that sounds like it might hurt. Maybe there's no milkshake involved.
!

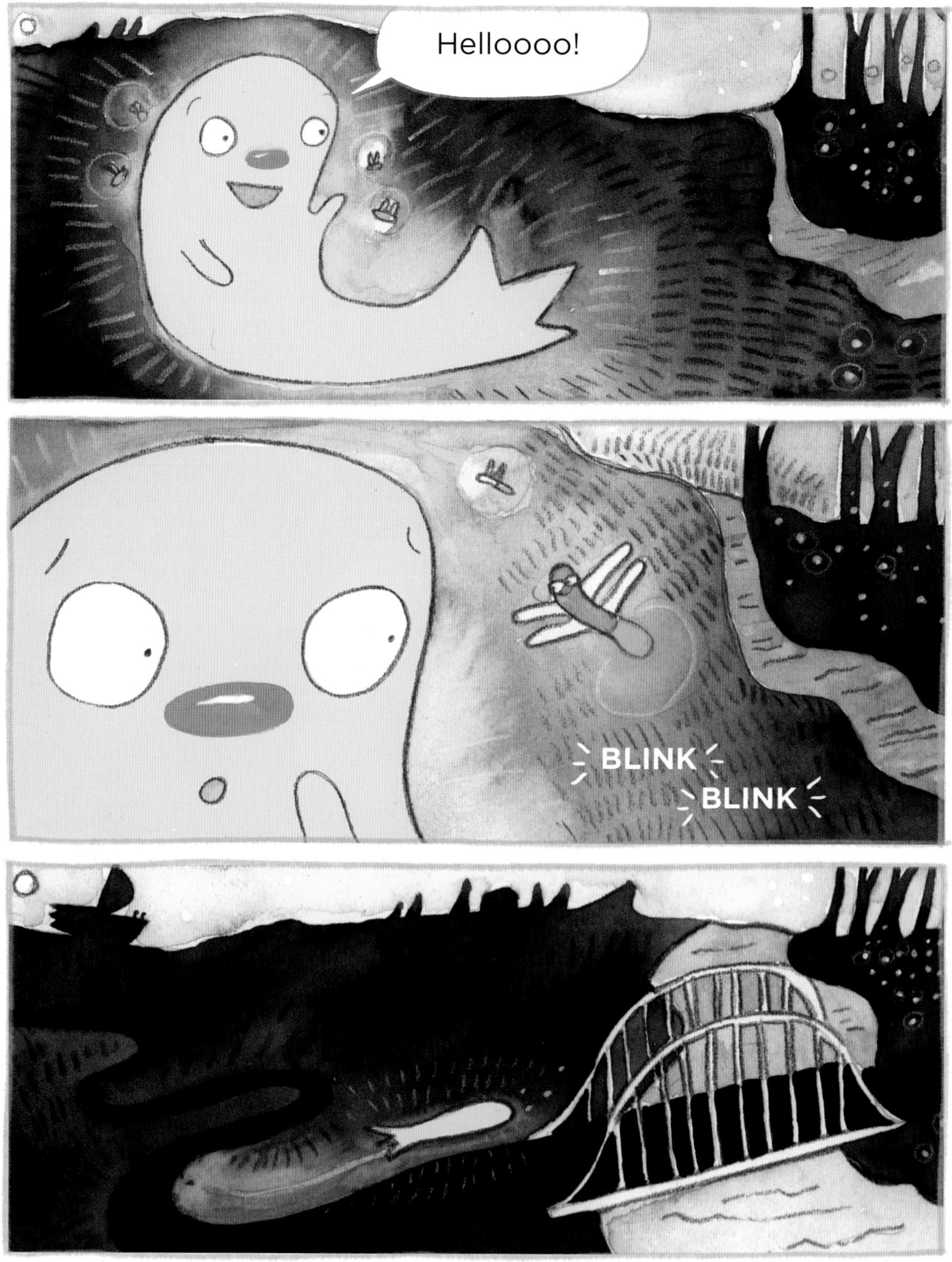
Helloooo!
BLINK
BLINK

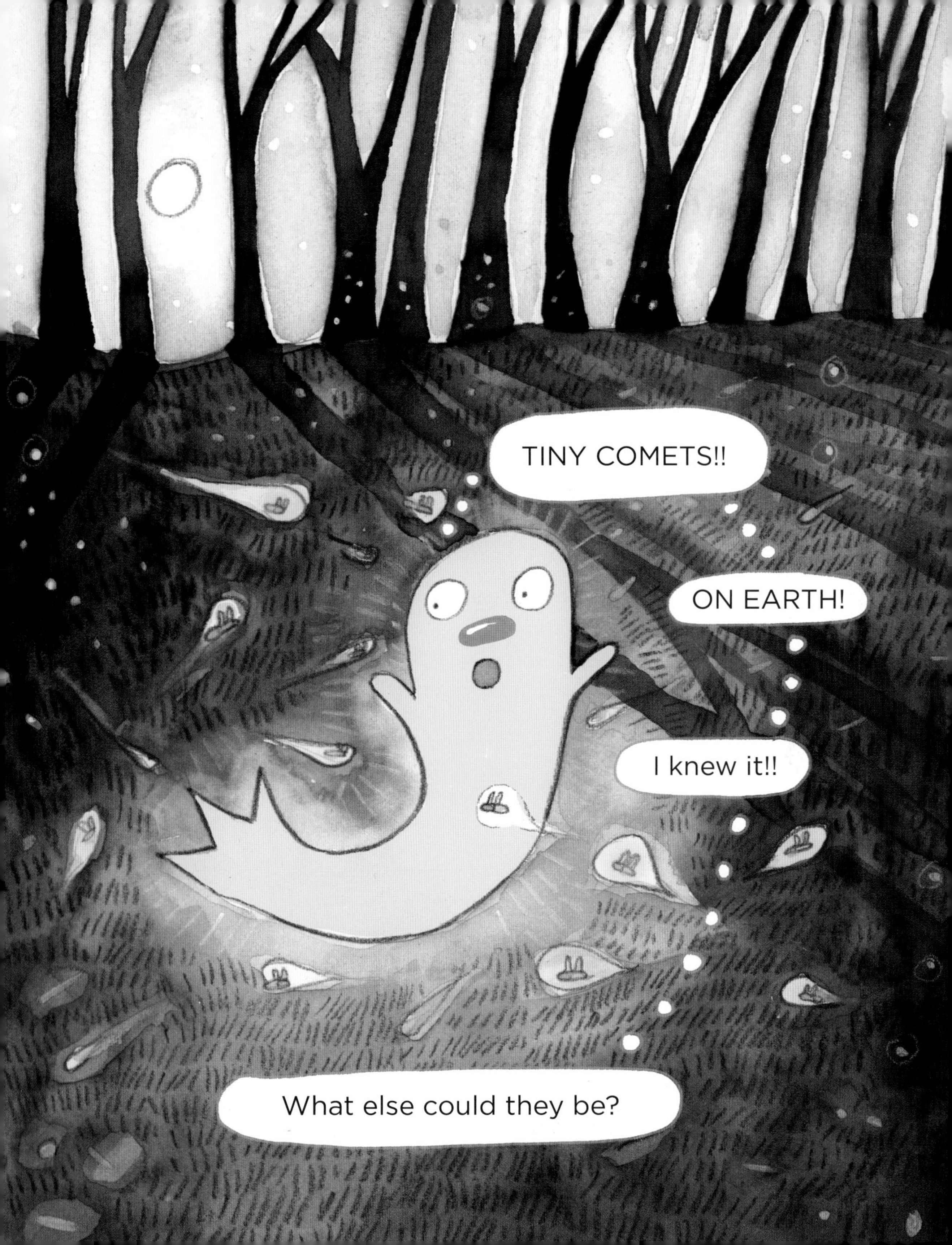
TINY COMETS!!
ON EARTH!
I knew it!!
What else could they be?

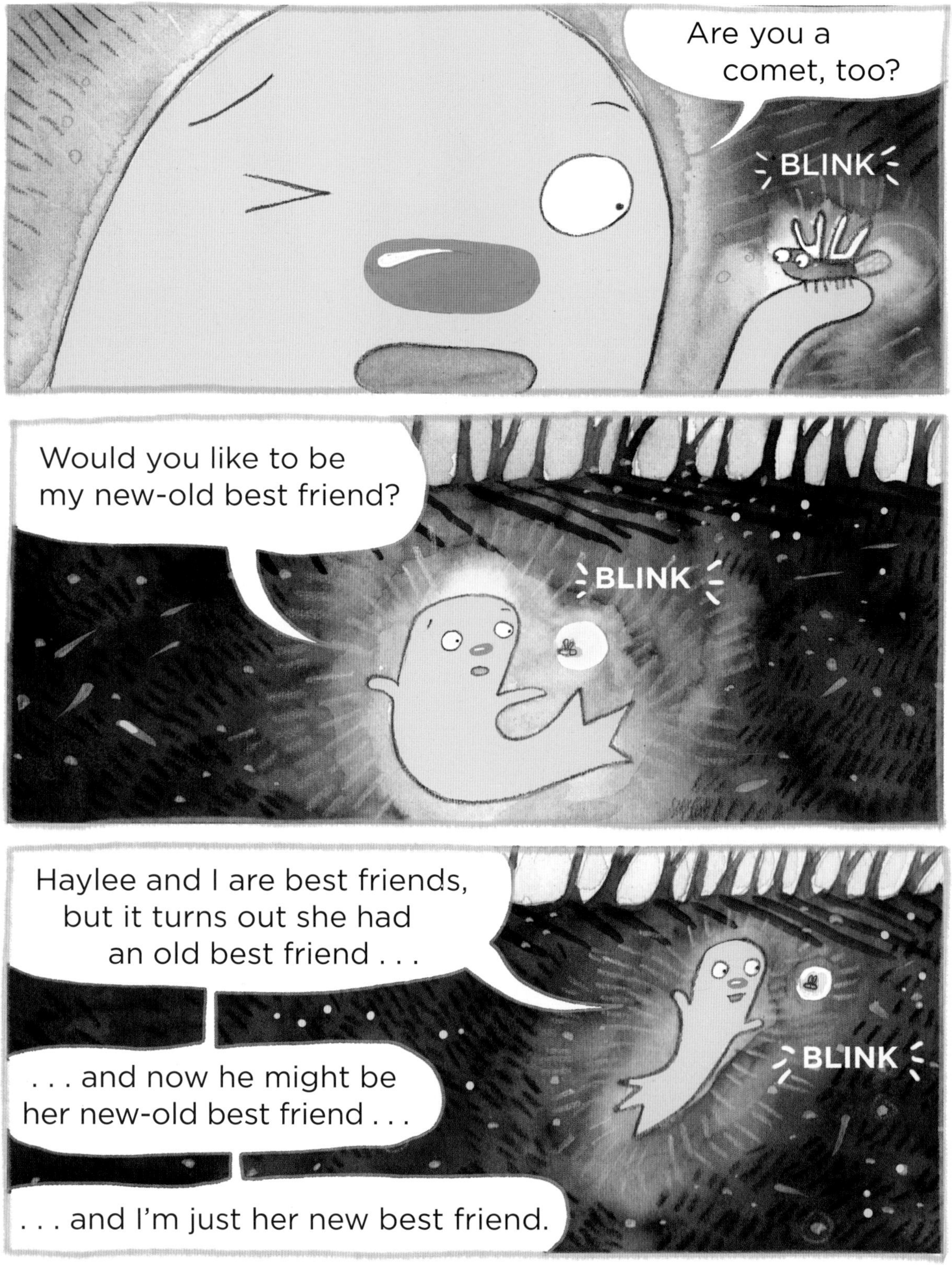
Are you a comet, too?
BLINK
Would you like to be my new-old best friend?
BLINK
Haylee and I are best friends, but it turns out she had an old best friend . . .
. . . and now he might be her new-old best friend . . .
. . . and I'm just her new best friend.
BLINK

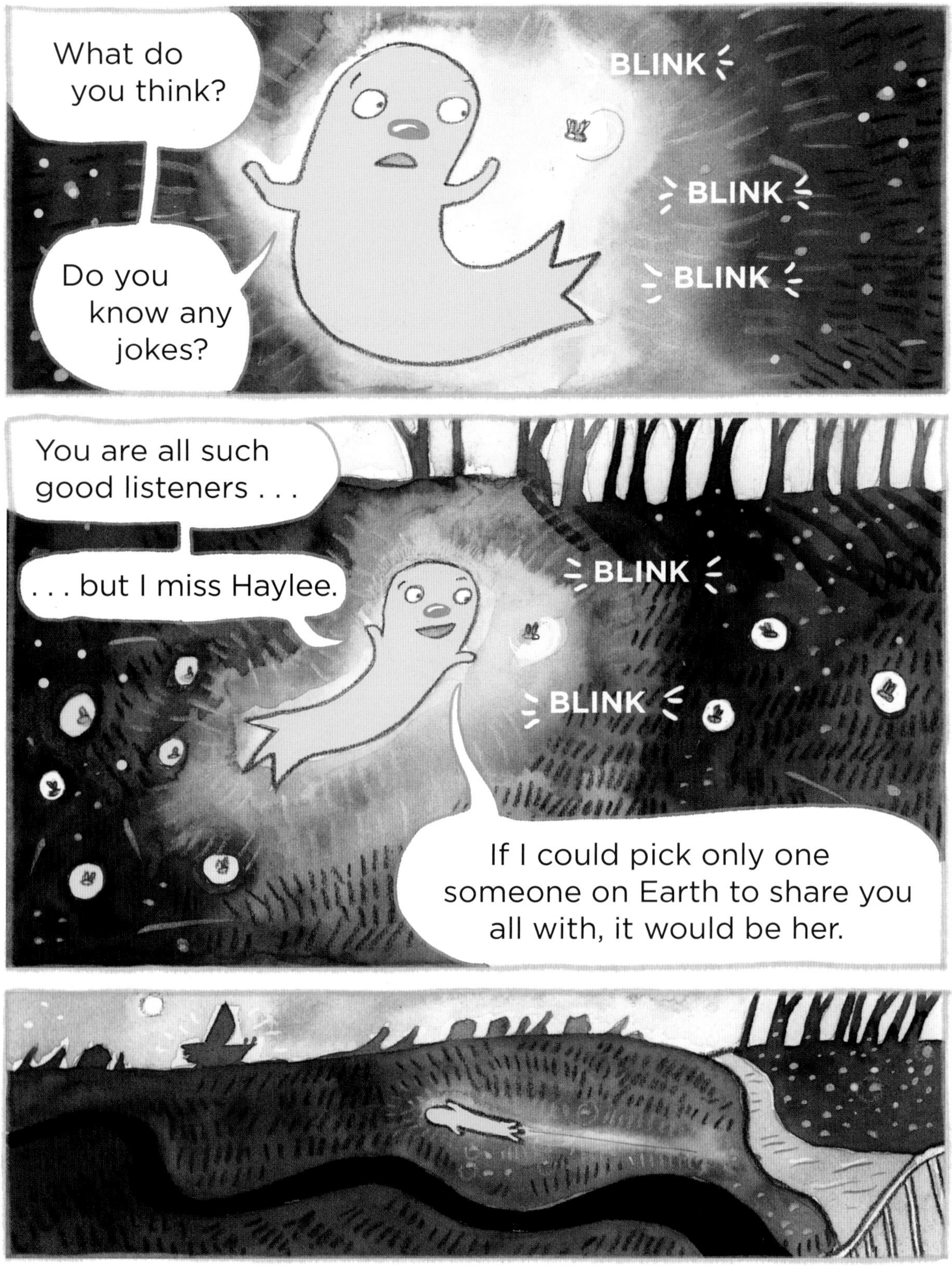

What do you think?
Do you know any jokes?
BLINK
BLINK
BLINK
You are all such good listeners . . .
. . . but I miss Haylee.
BLINK
BLINK
If I could pick only one someone on Earth to share you all with, it would be her.

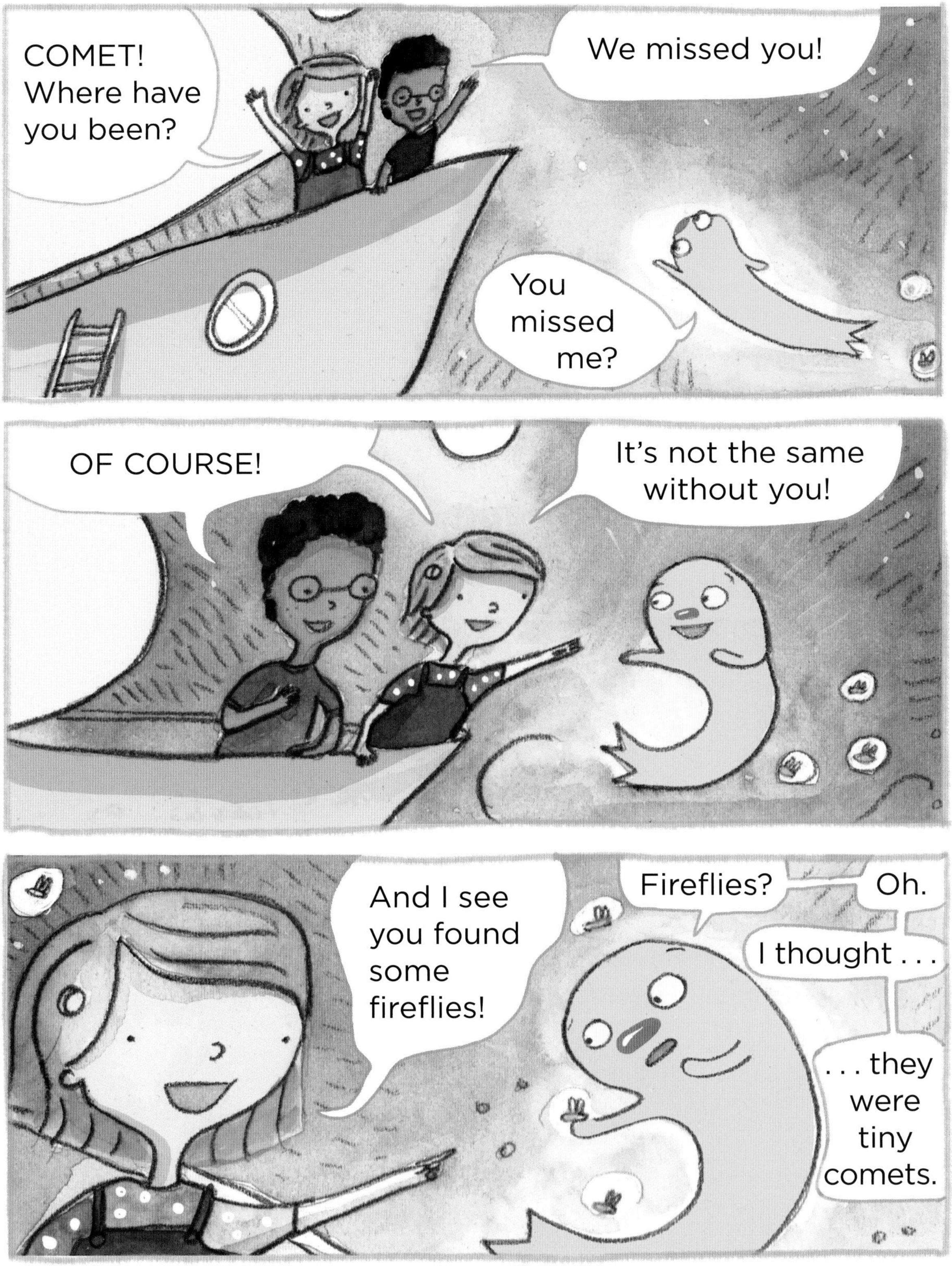
COMET! Where have you been?
We missed you!
You missed me?
OF COURSE!
It's not the same without you!
And I see you found some fireflies!
Fireflies?
Oh.
I thought . . .
. . . they were tiny comets.

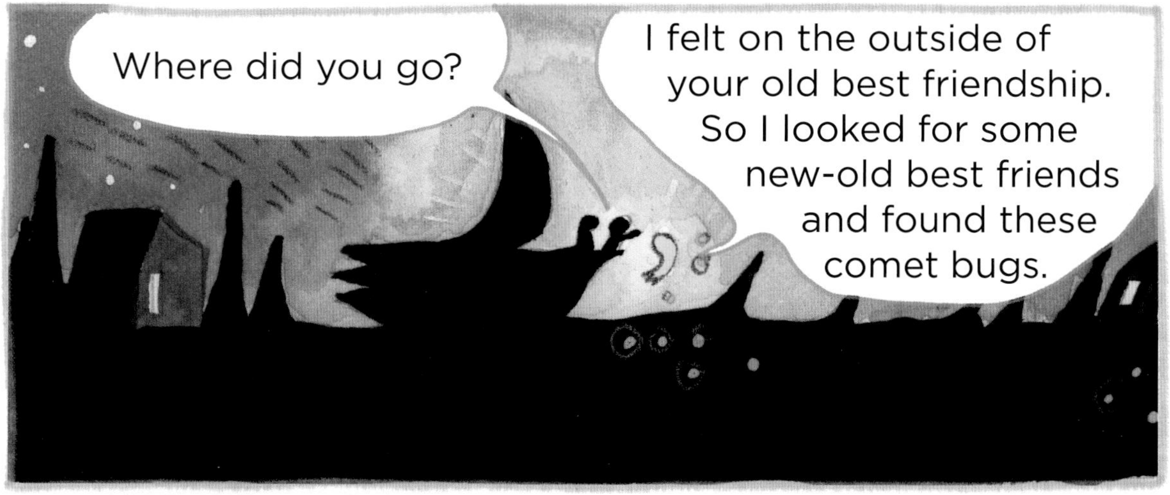
Where did you go?
I felt on the outside of your old best friendship. So I looked for some new-old best friends and found these comet bugs.

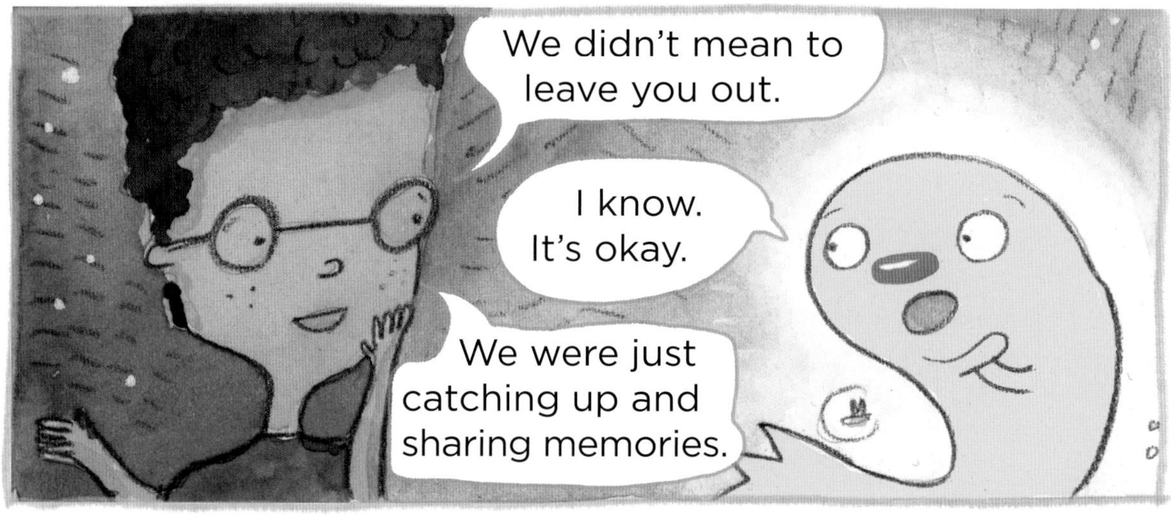
We didn't mean to leave you out.
I know. It's okay.
We were just catching up and sharing memories.

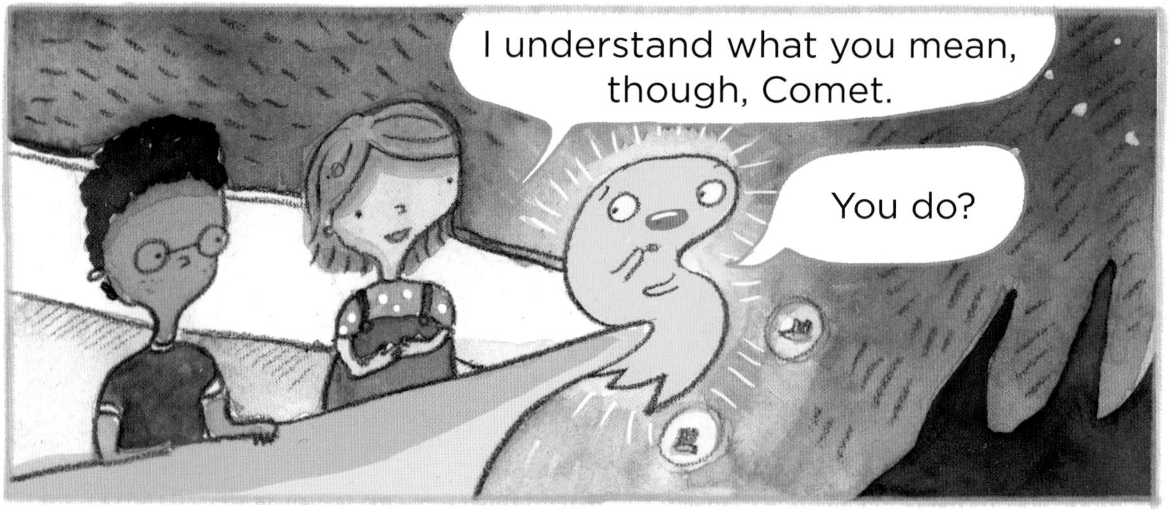
I understand what you mean, though, Comet.
You do?

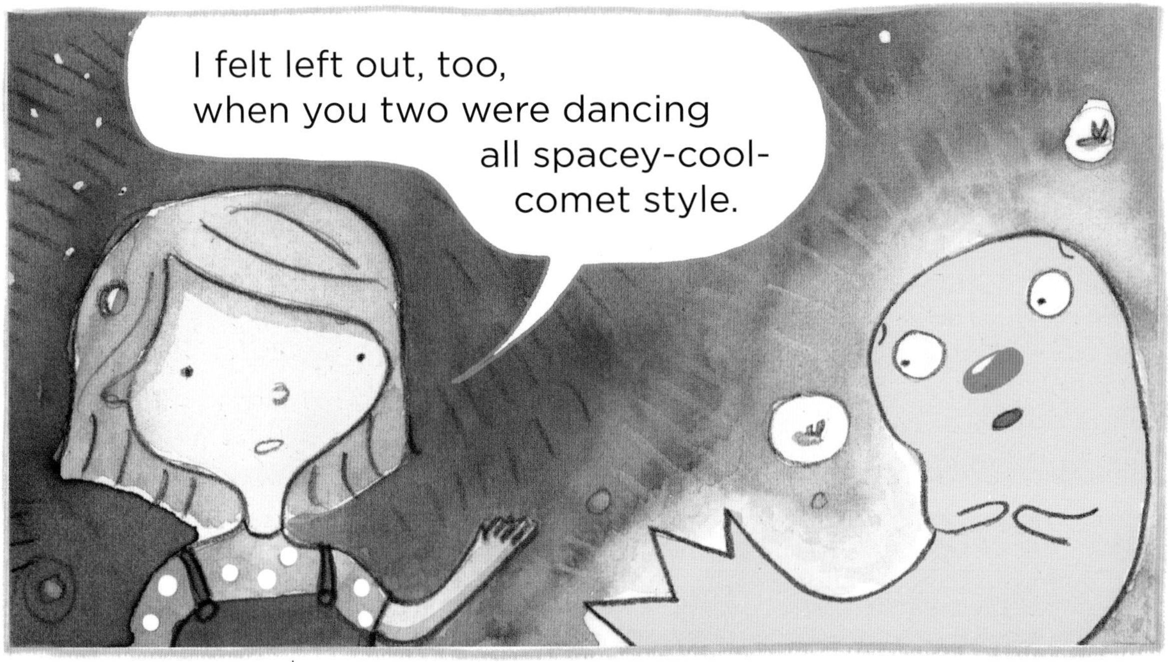
I felt left out, too, when you two were dancing all spacey-cool-comet style.

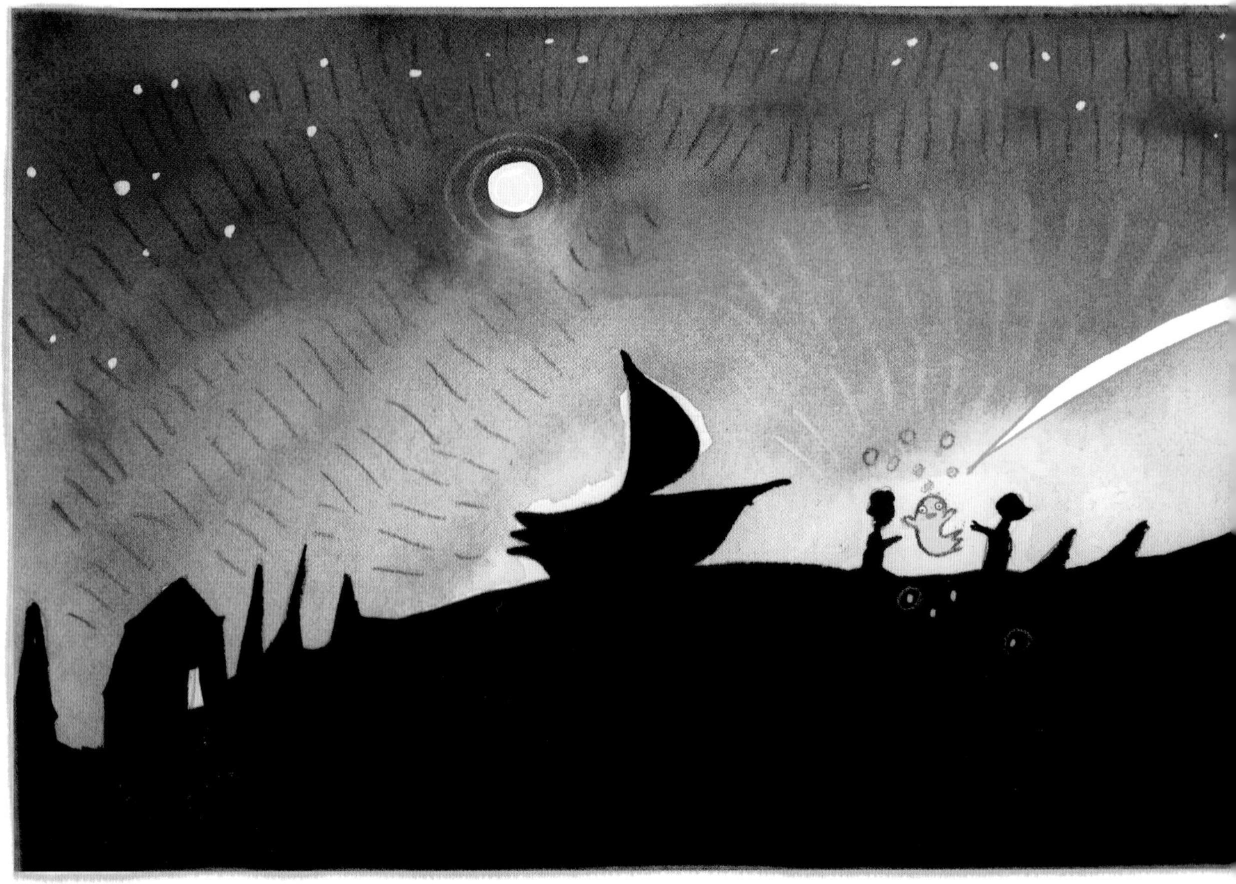

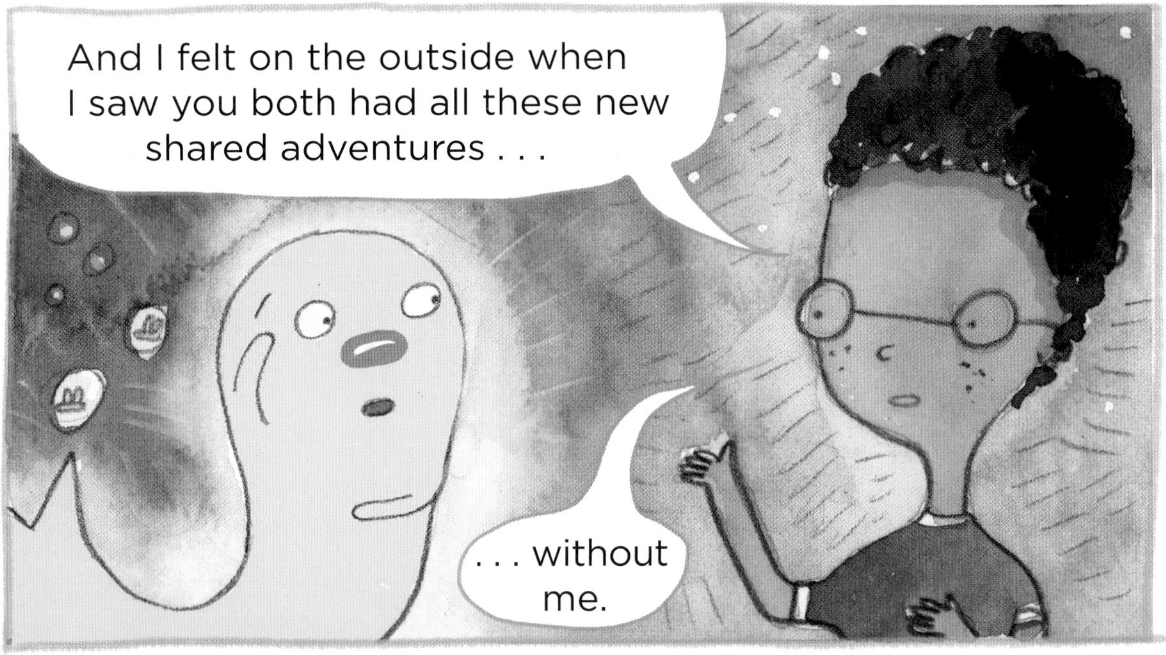
And I felt on the outside when I saw you both had all these new shared adventures . . .
. . . without me.

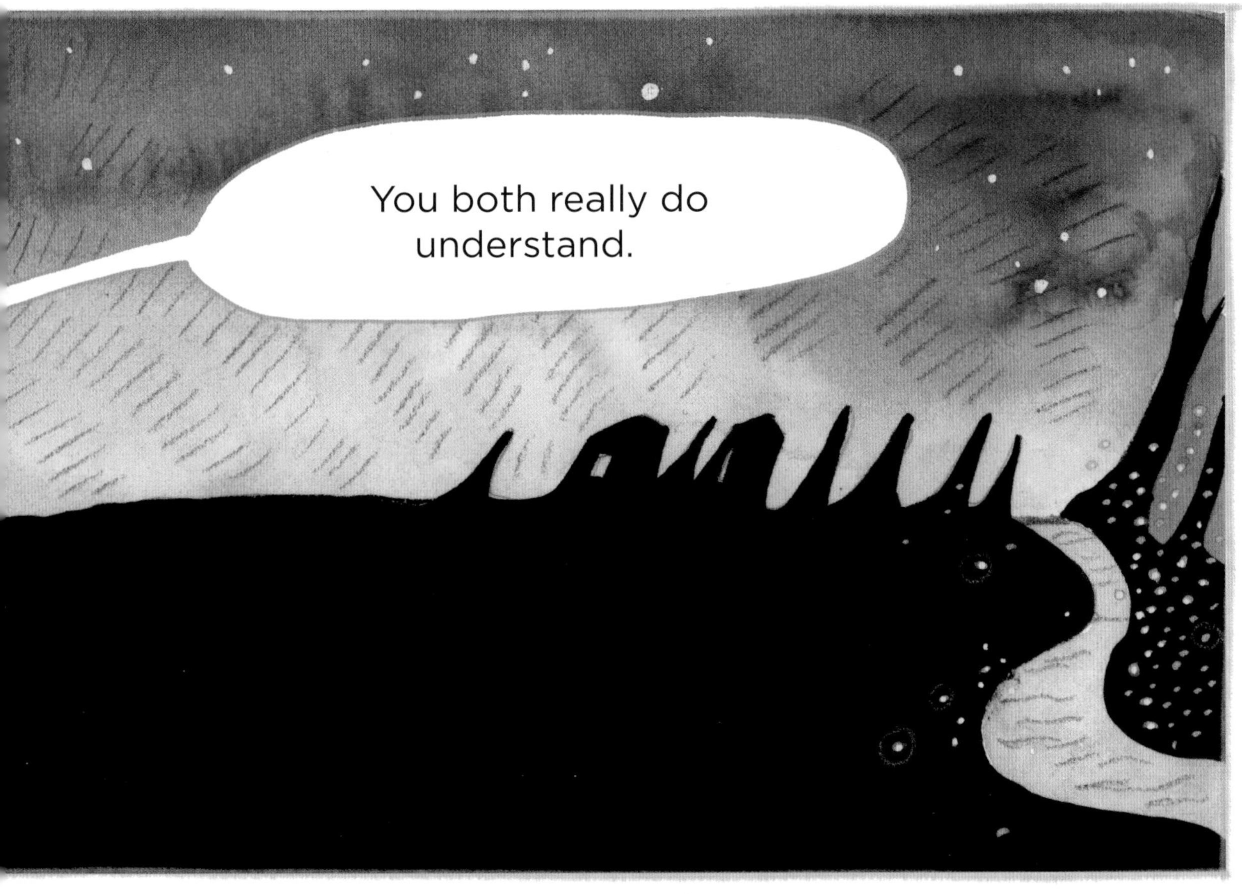
You both really do understand.

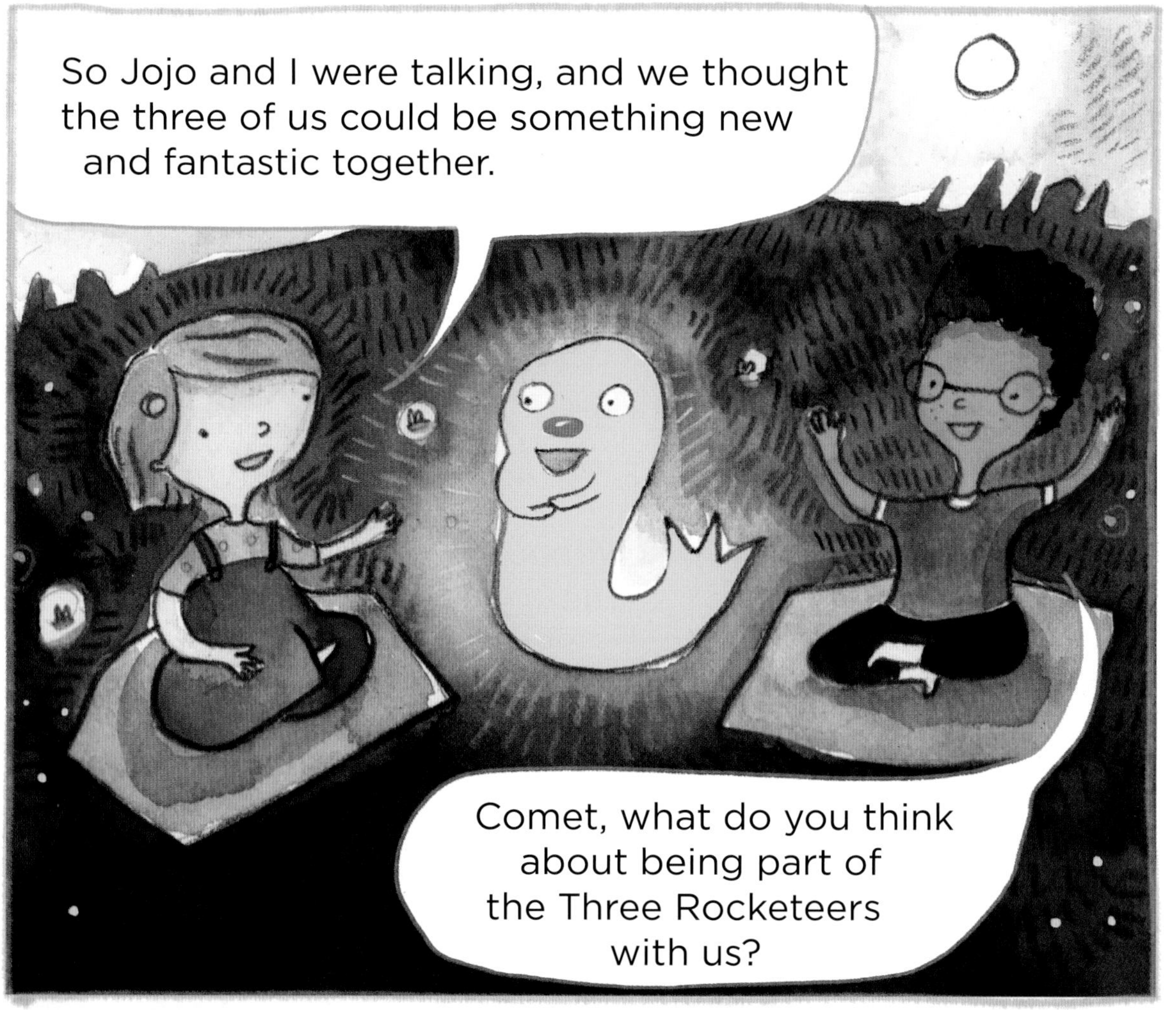
So Jojo and I were talking, and we thought the three of us could be something new and fantastic together.
Comet, what do you think about being part of the Three Rocketeers with us?

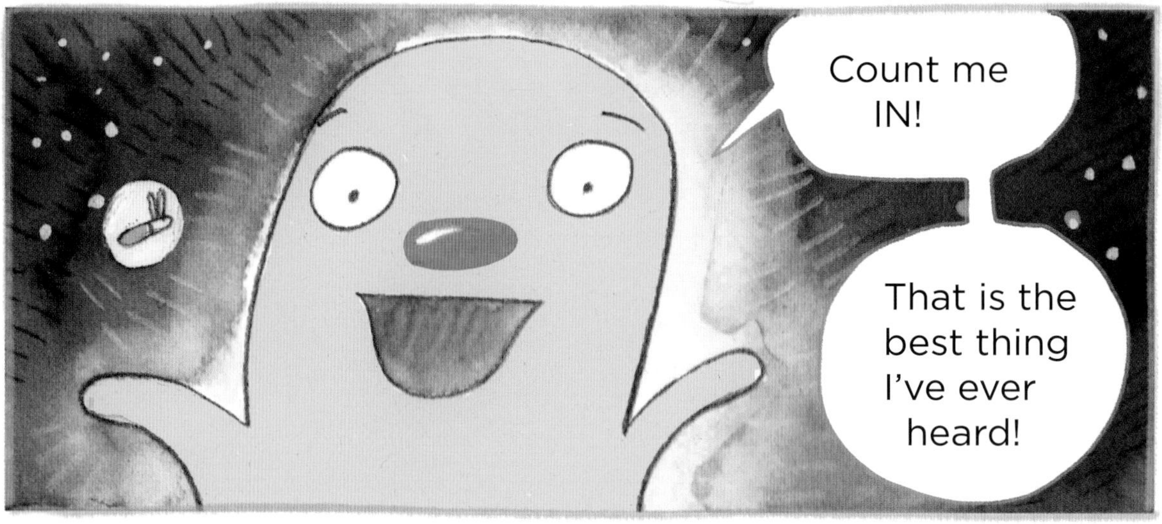
Count me IN!
That is the best thing I've ever heard!

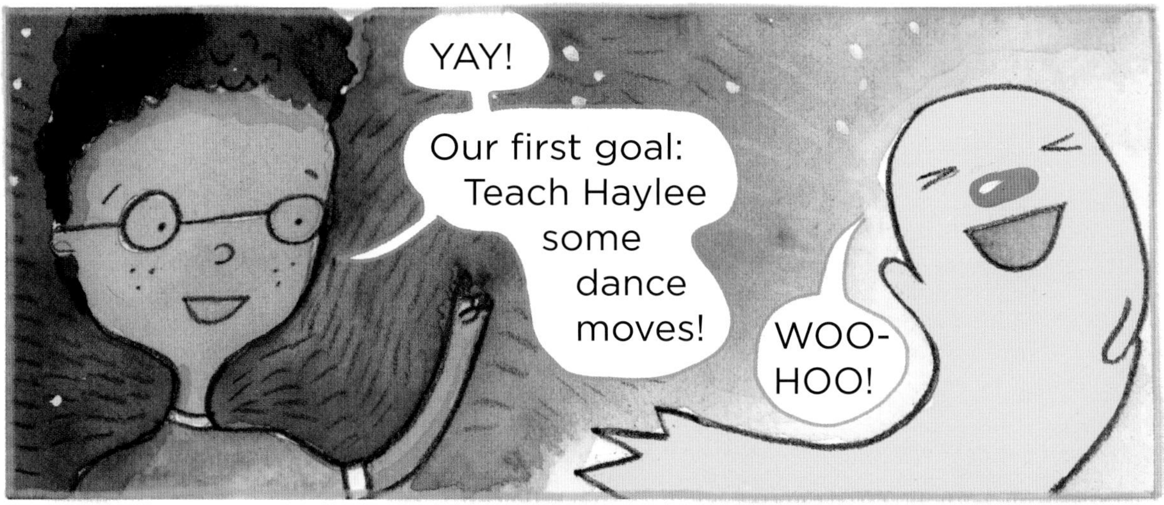
YAY!
Our first goal: Teach Haylee some dance moves!
WOO-HOO!

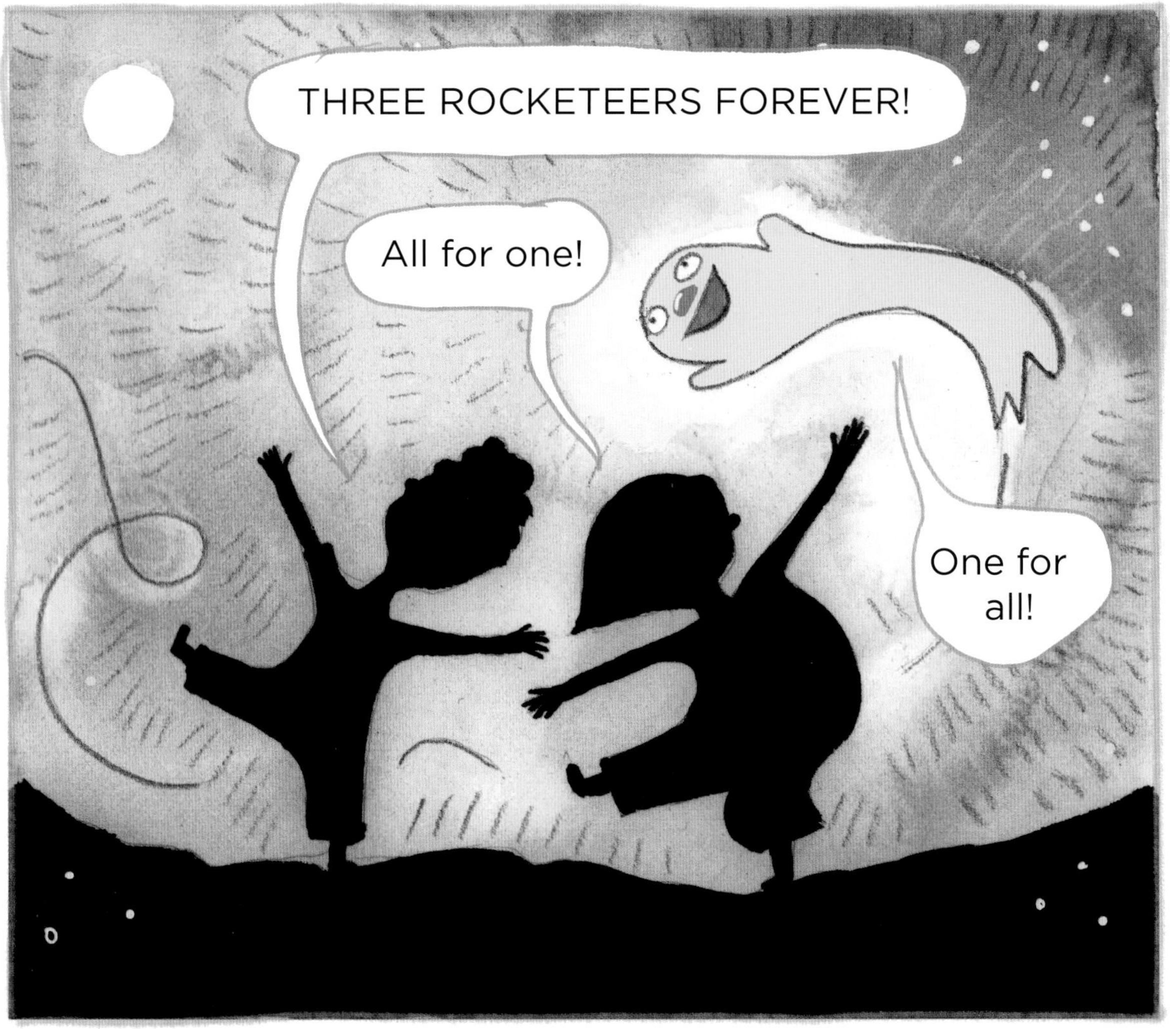
THREE ROCKETEERS FOREVER!
All for one!
One for all!

# FIREFLIES VS. COMETS

1. Definition:

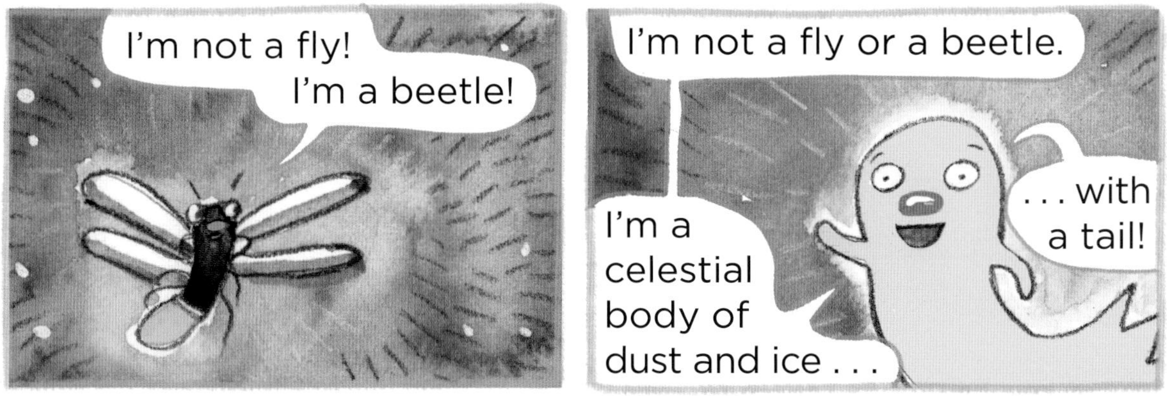
I'm not a fly! I'm a beetle!
I'm not a fly or a beetle.
I'm a celestial body of dust and ice . . .
. . . with a tail!

2. Glow style:

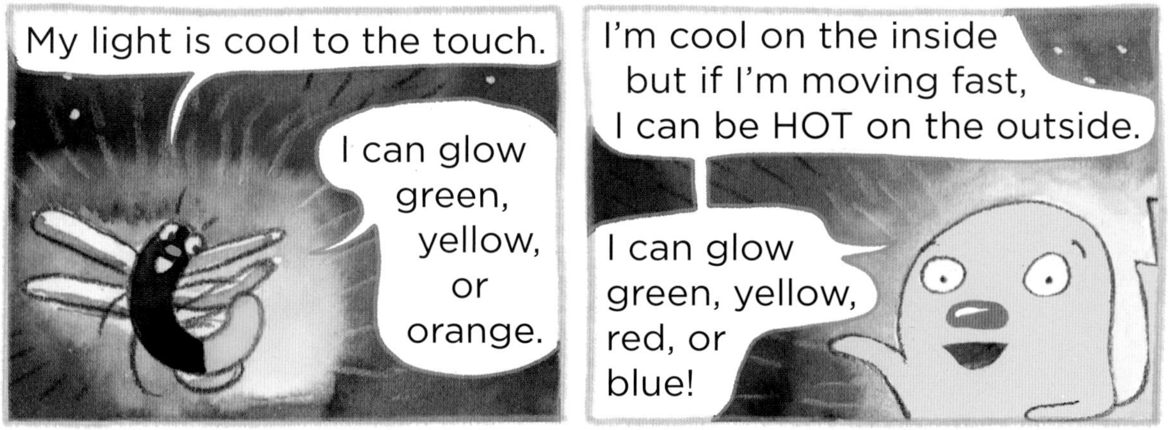
My light is cool to the touch.
I can glow green, yellow, or orange.
I'm cool on the inside but if I'm moving fast, I can be HOT on the outside.
I can glow green, yellow, red, or blue!

3. Communication style:

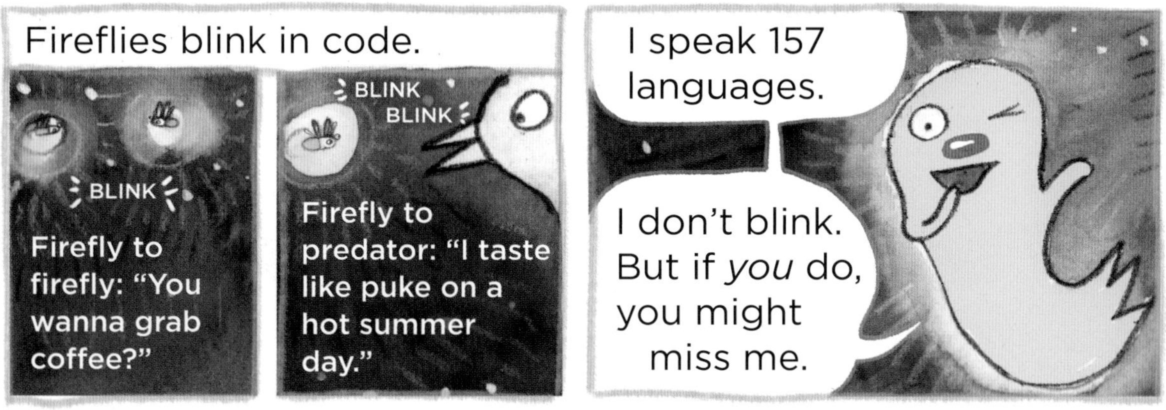
Fireflies blink in code.
BLINK
Firefly to firefly: "You wanna grab coffee?"
BLINK
BLINK
Firefly to predator: "I taste like puke on a hot summer day."
I speak 157 languages.
I don't blink. But if *you* do, you might miss me.

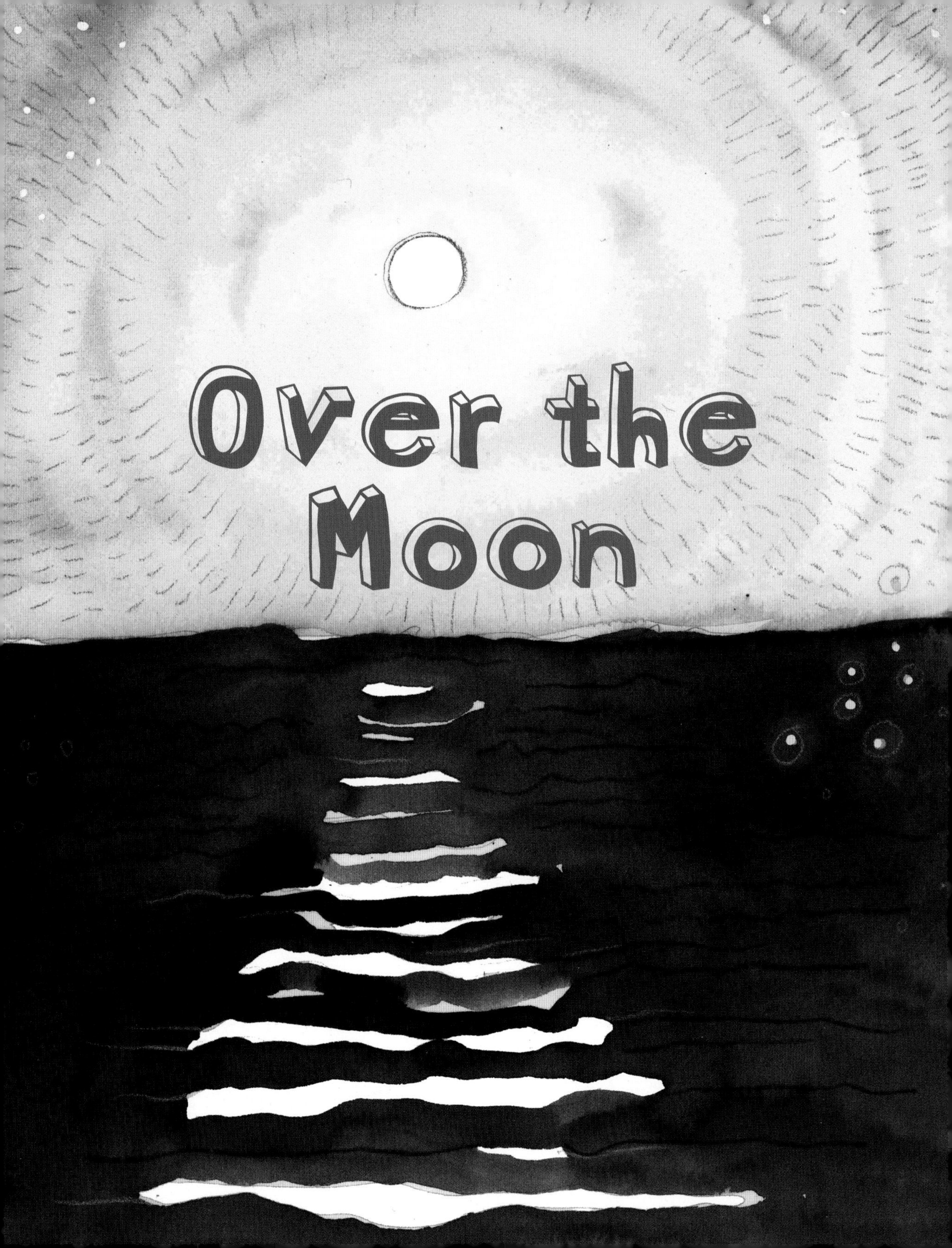
Over the
Moon

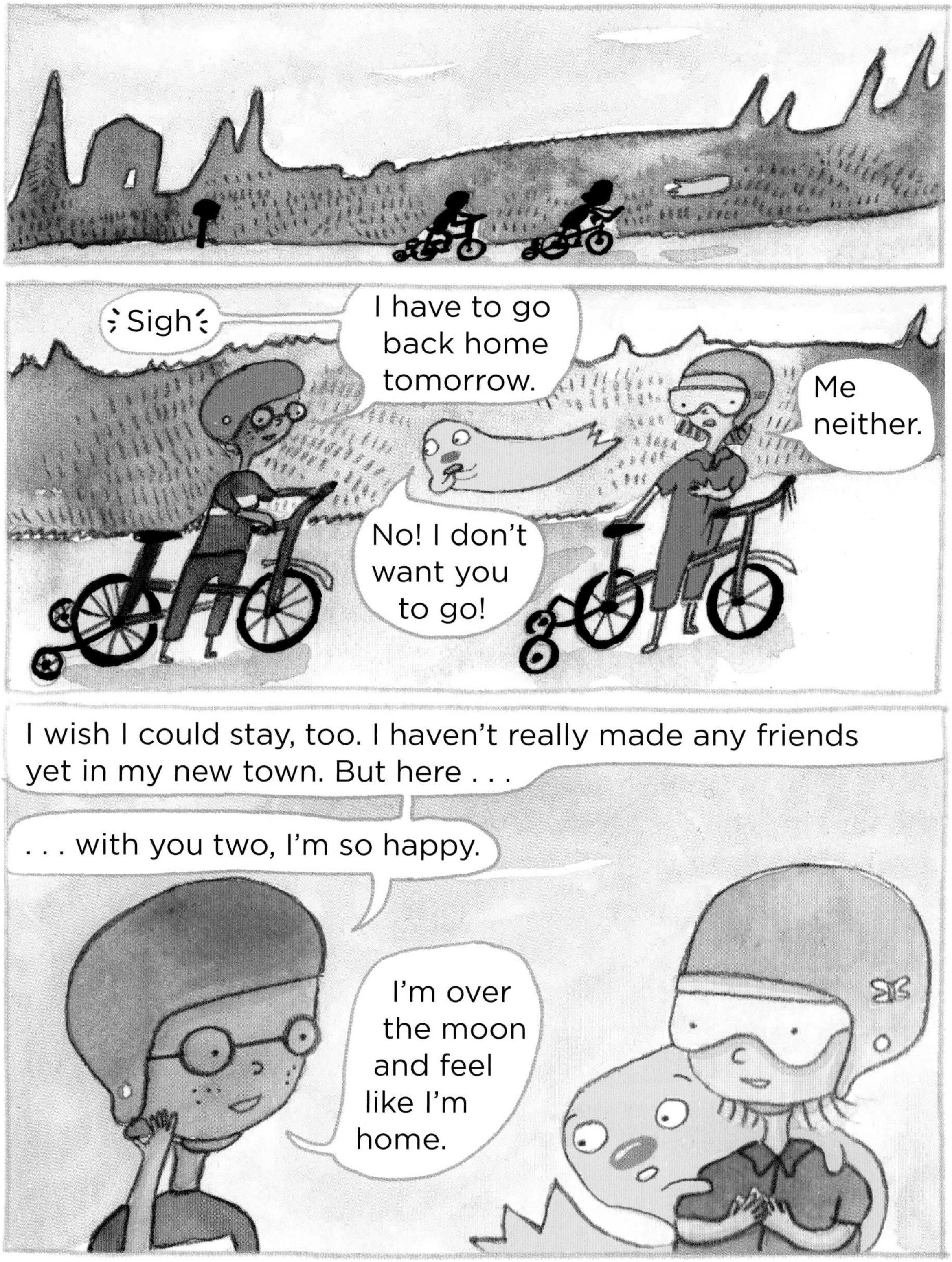
Sigh
I have to go back home tomorrow.
Me neither.
No! I don't want you to go!
I wish I could stay, too. I haven't really made any friends yet in my new town. But here . . .
. . . with you two, I'm so happy.
I'm over the moon and feel like I'm home.

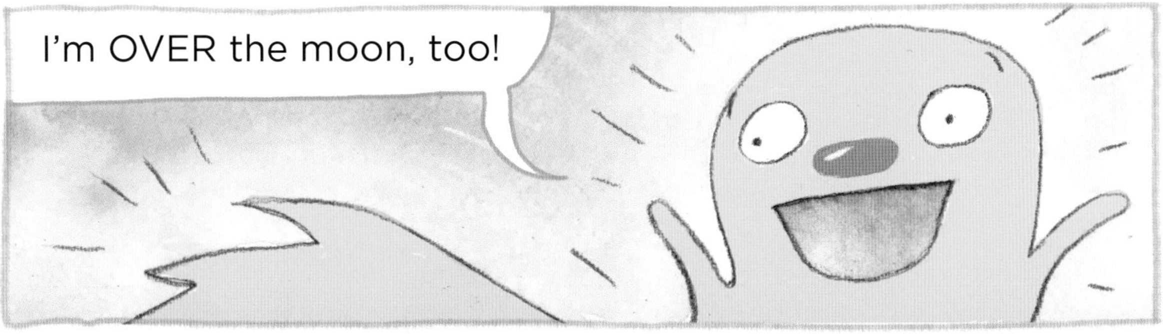
I'm OVER the moon, too!

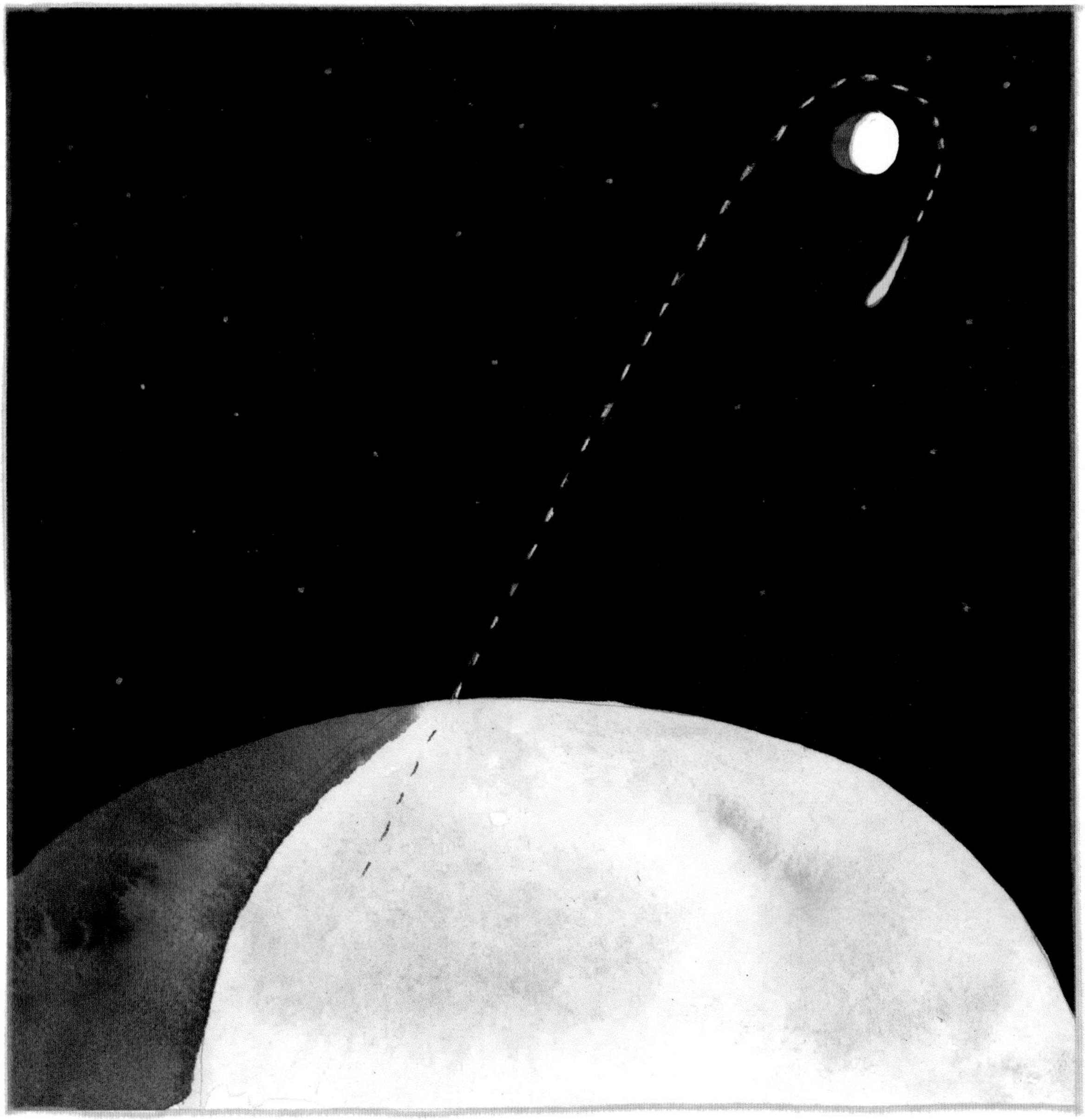

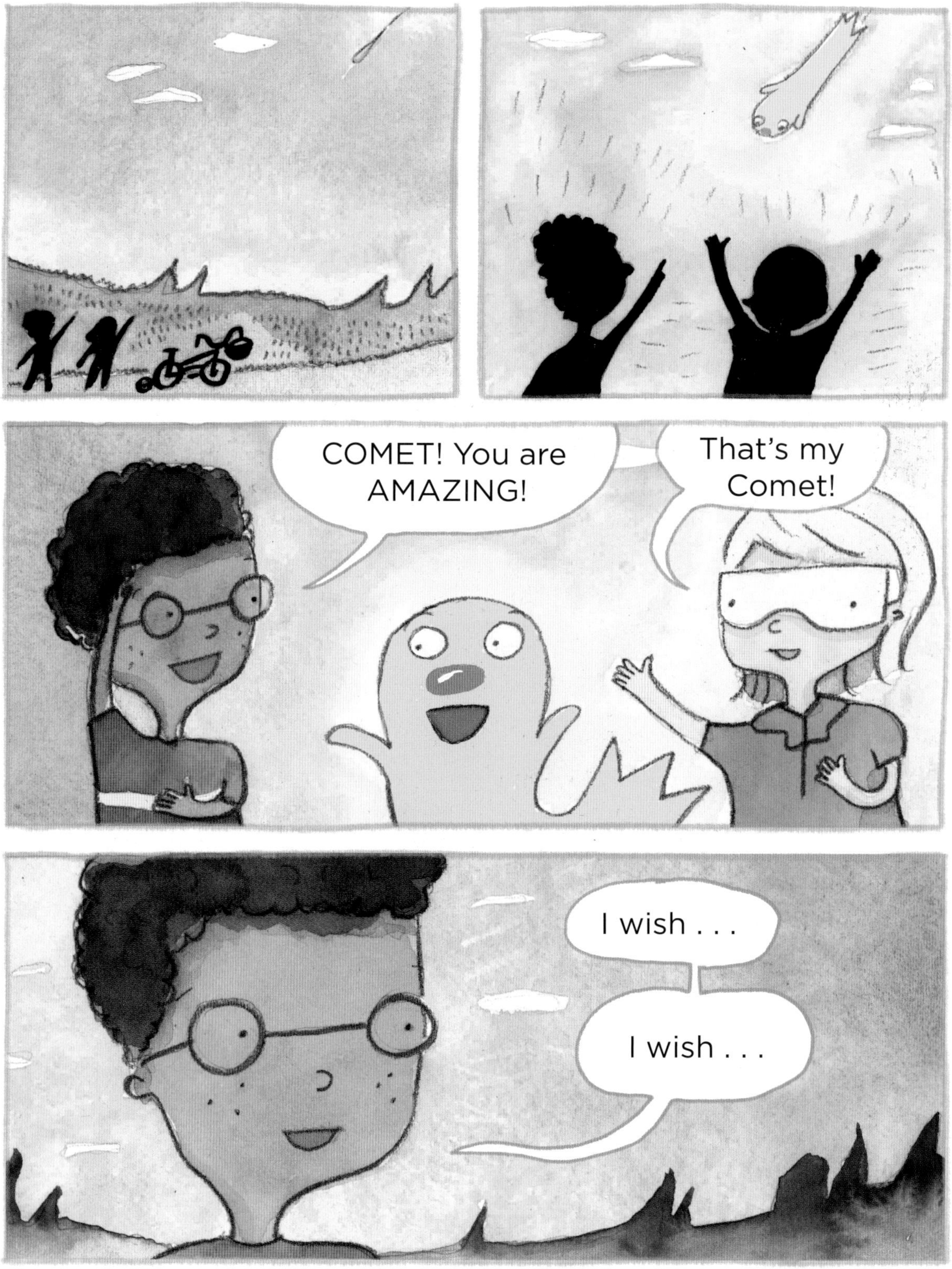
COMET! You are AMAZING!
That's my Comet!
I wish . . .
I wish . . .

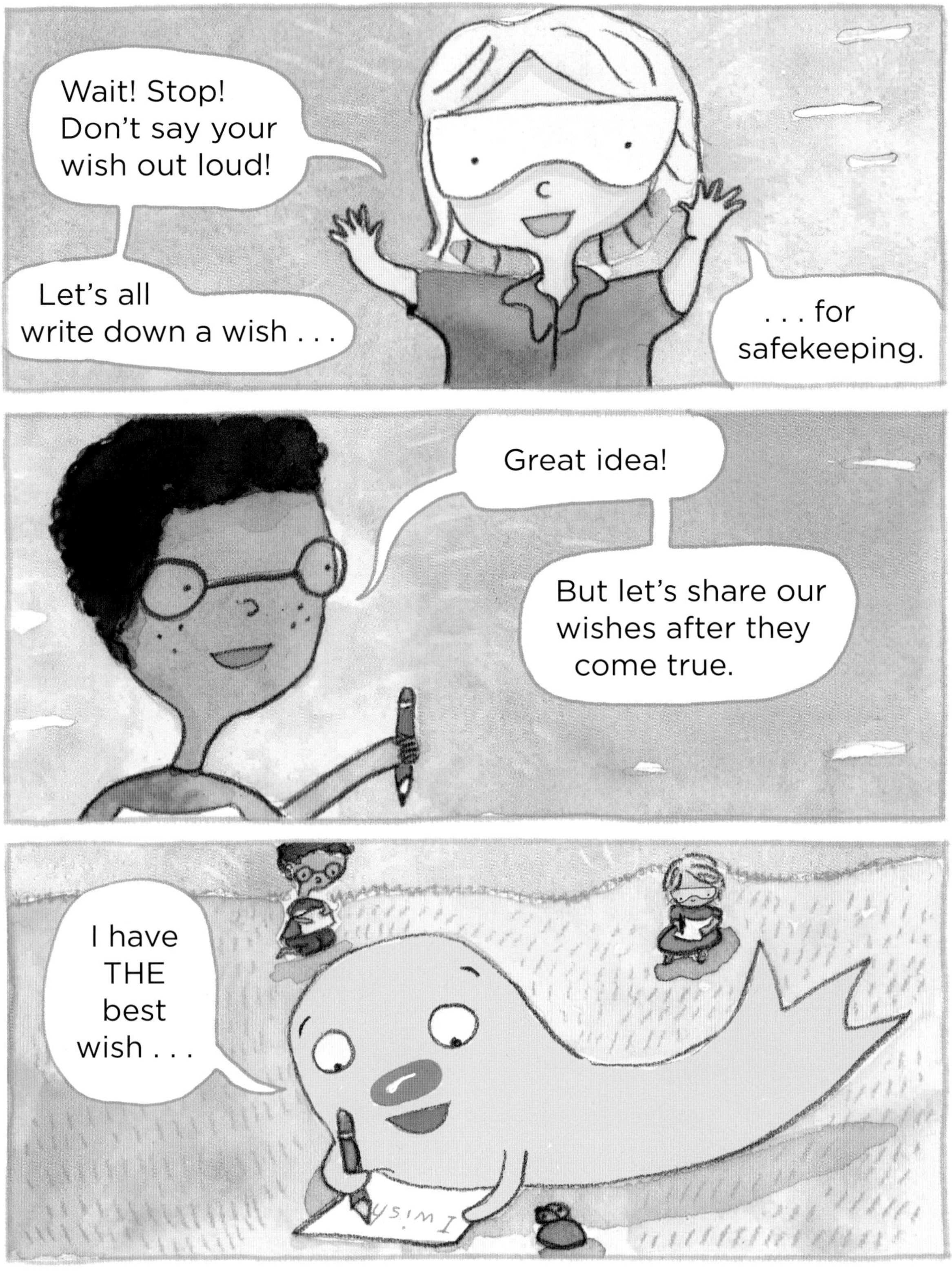
Wait! Stop! Don't say your wish out loud!
Let's all write down a wish . . .
. . . for safekeeping.
Great idea!
But let's share our wishes after they come true.
I have THE best wish . . .

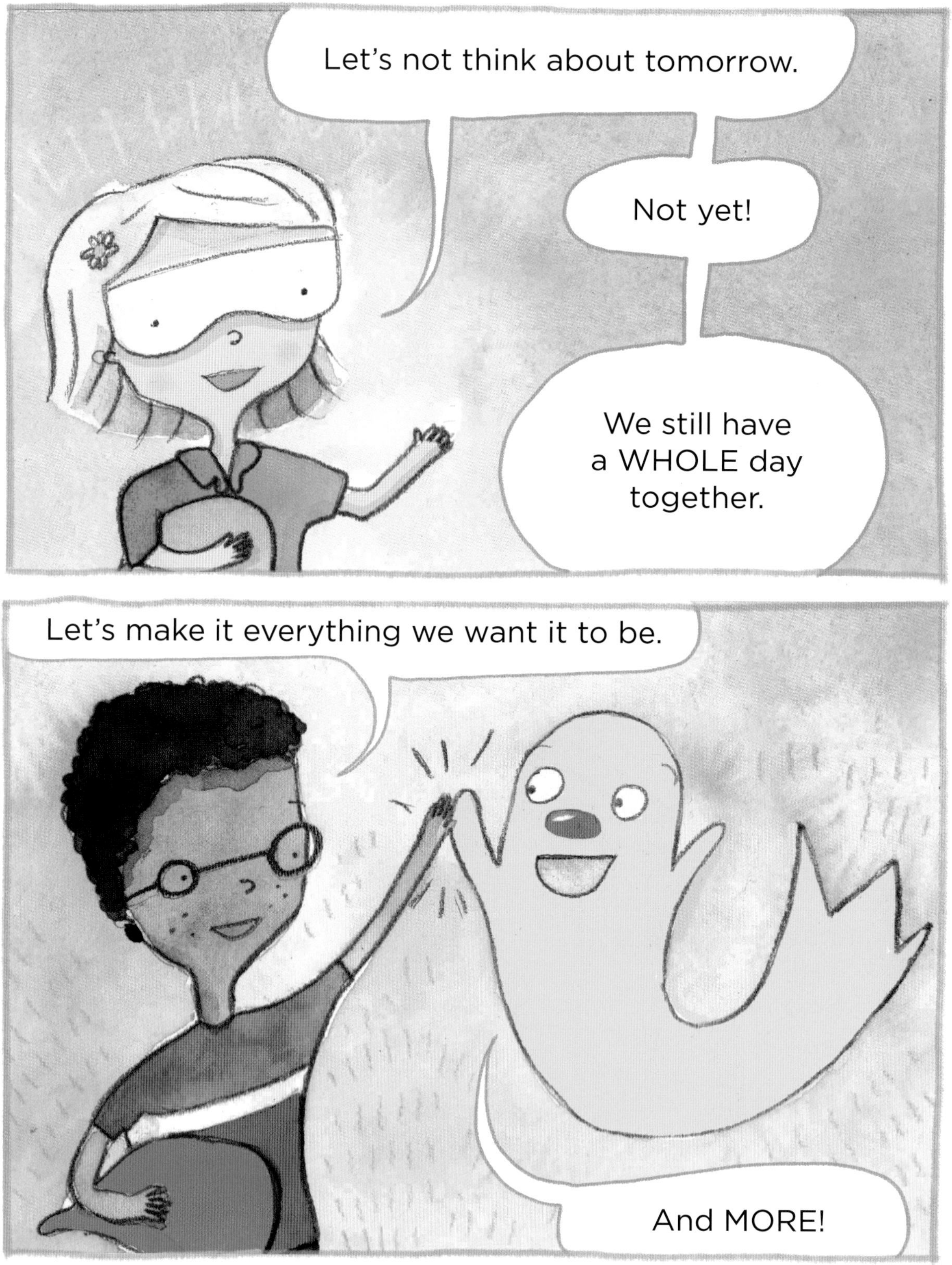

Let's not think about tomorrow.
Not yet!
We still have a WHOLE day together.
Let's make it everything we want it to be.
And MORE!

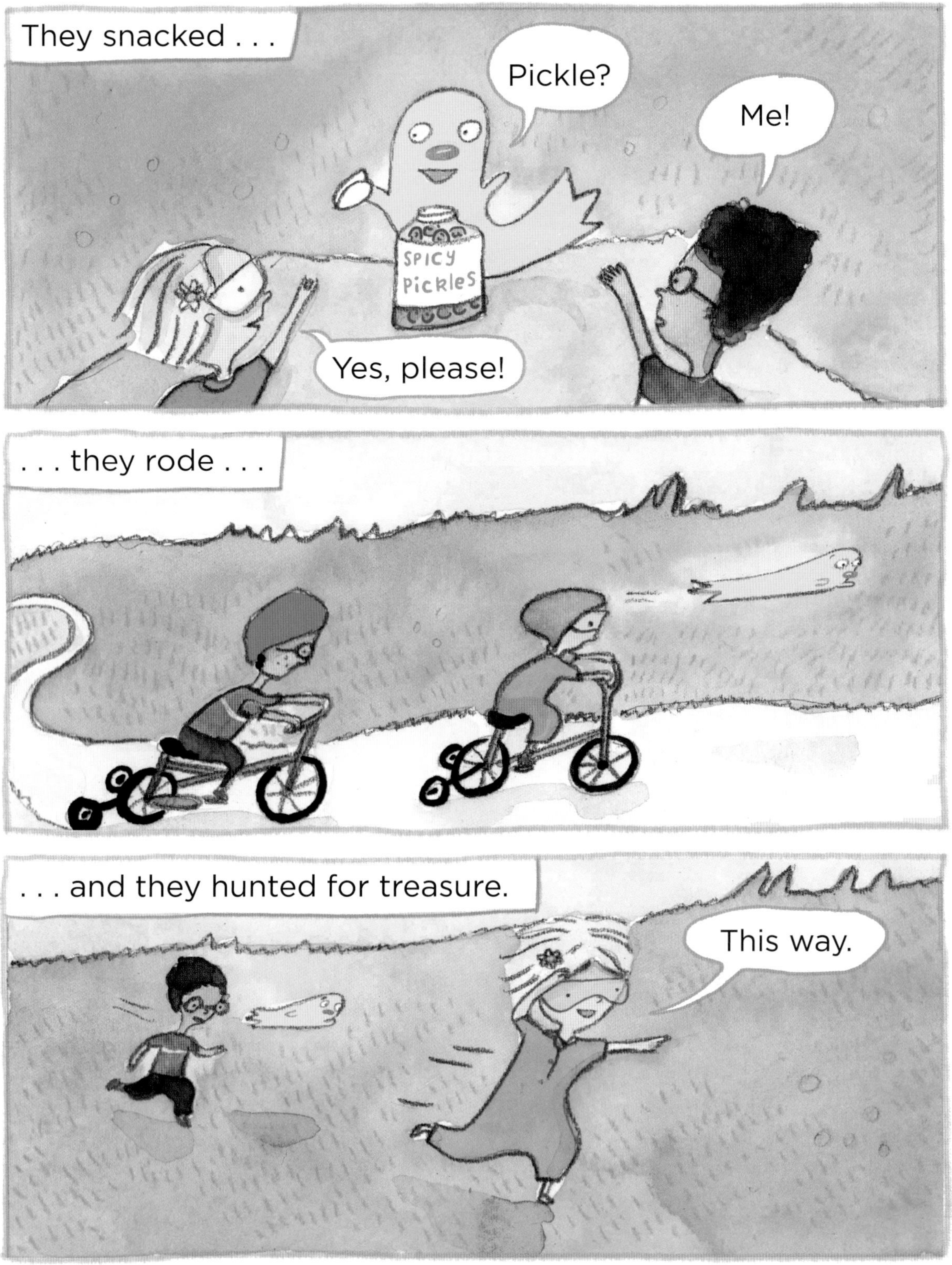
They snacked . . .
Pickle?
Me!
SPICY Pickles
Yes, please!
. . . they rode . . .
. . . and they hunted for treasure.
This way.

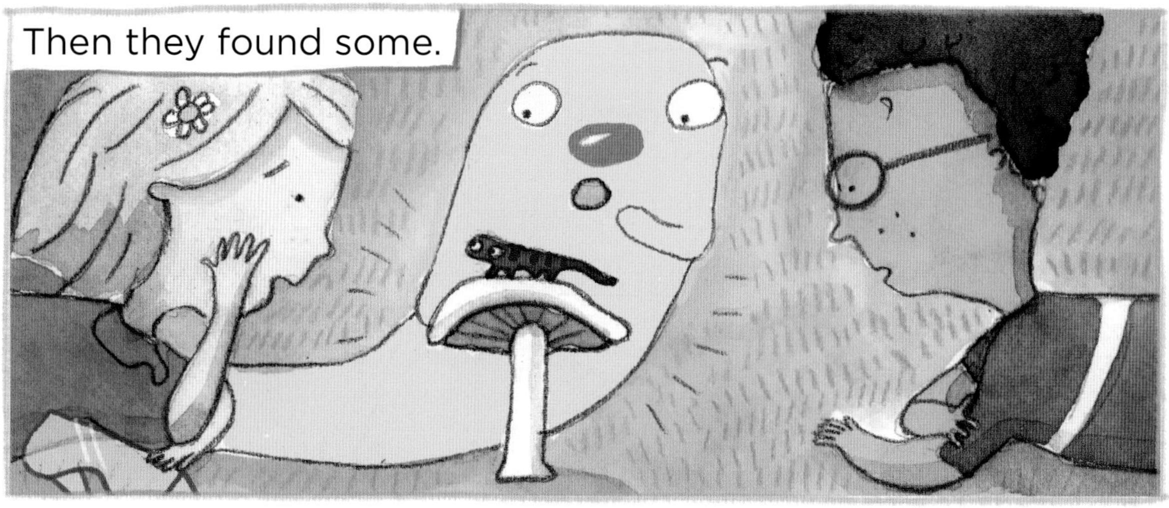
Then they found some.

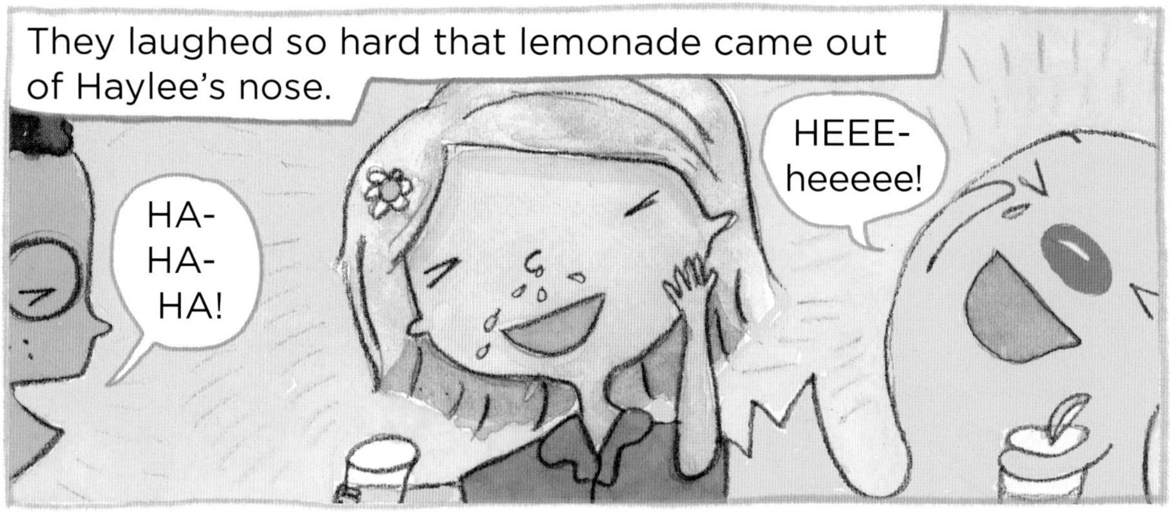
They laughed so hard that lemonade came out of Haylee's nose.
HA-HA-HA!
HEEE-heeeee!

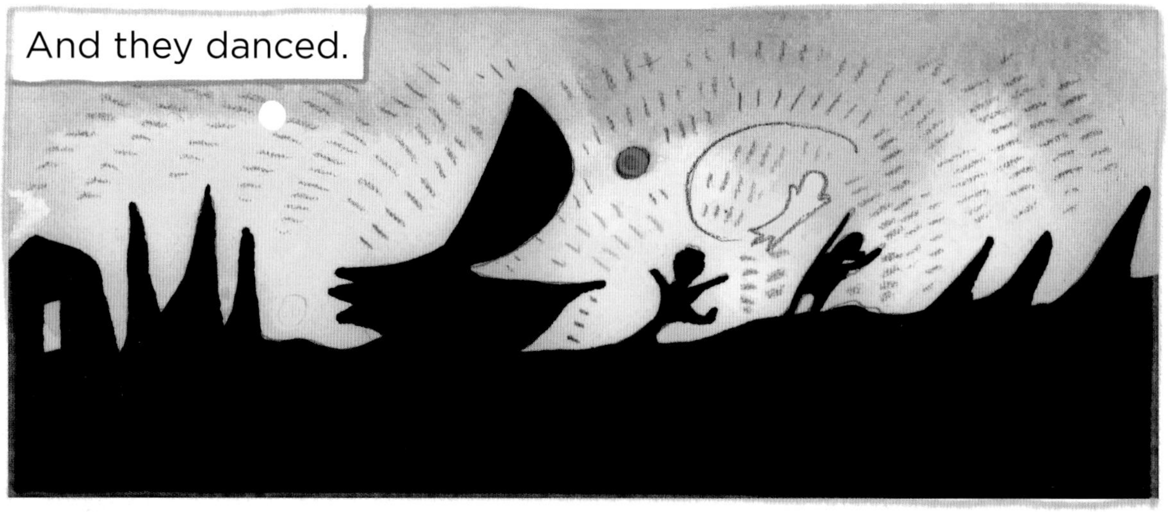
And they danced.

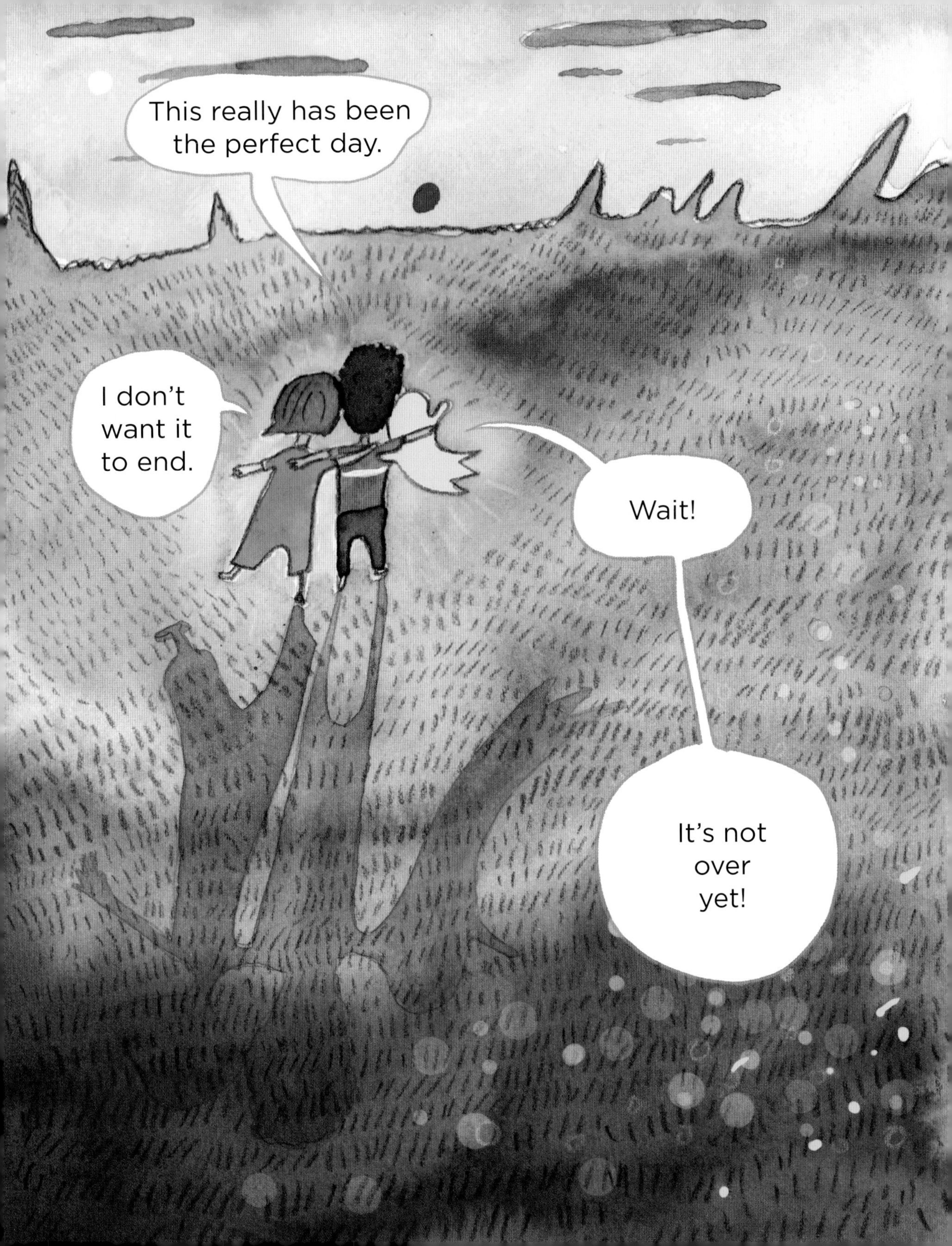
This really has been the perfect day.
I don't want it to end.
Wait!
It's not over yet!

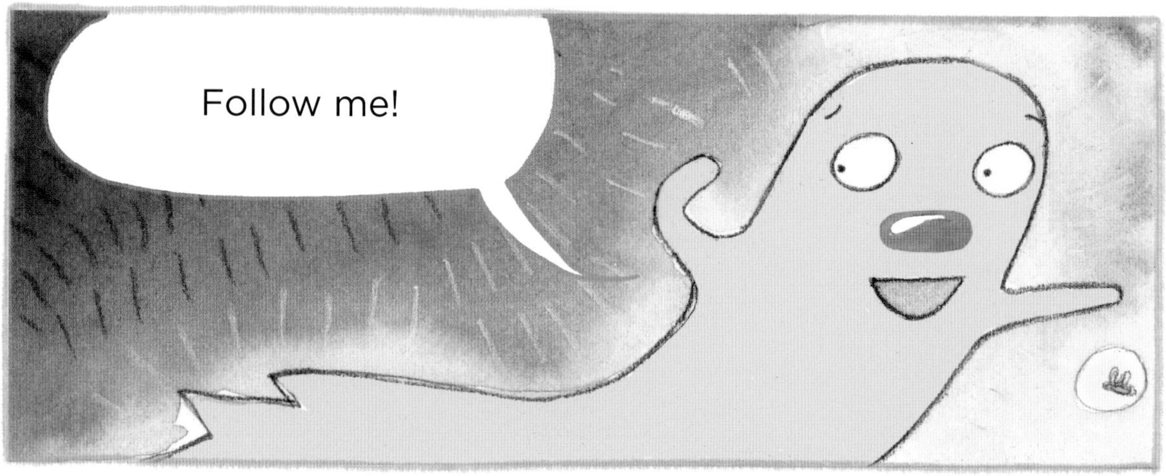
Follow me!

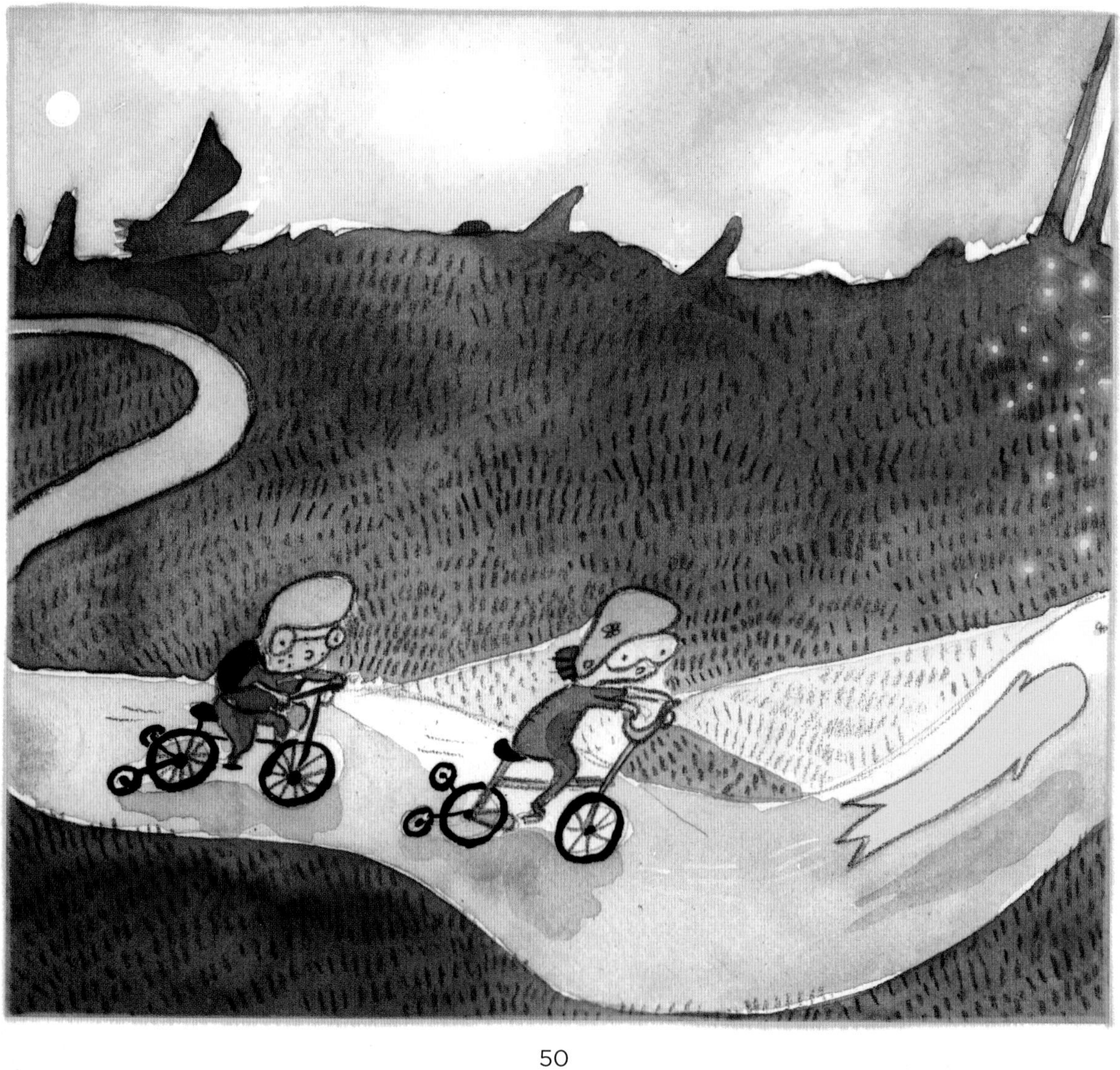

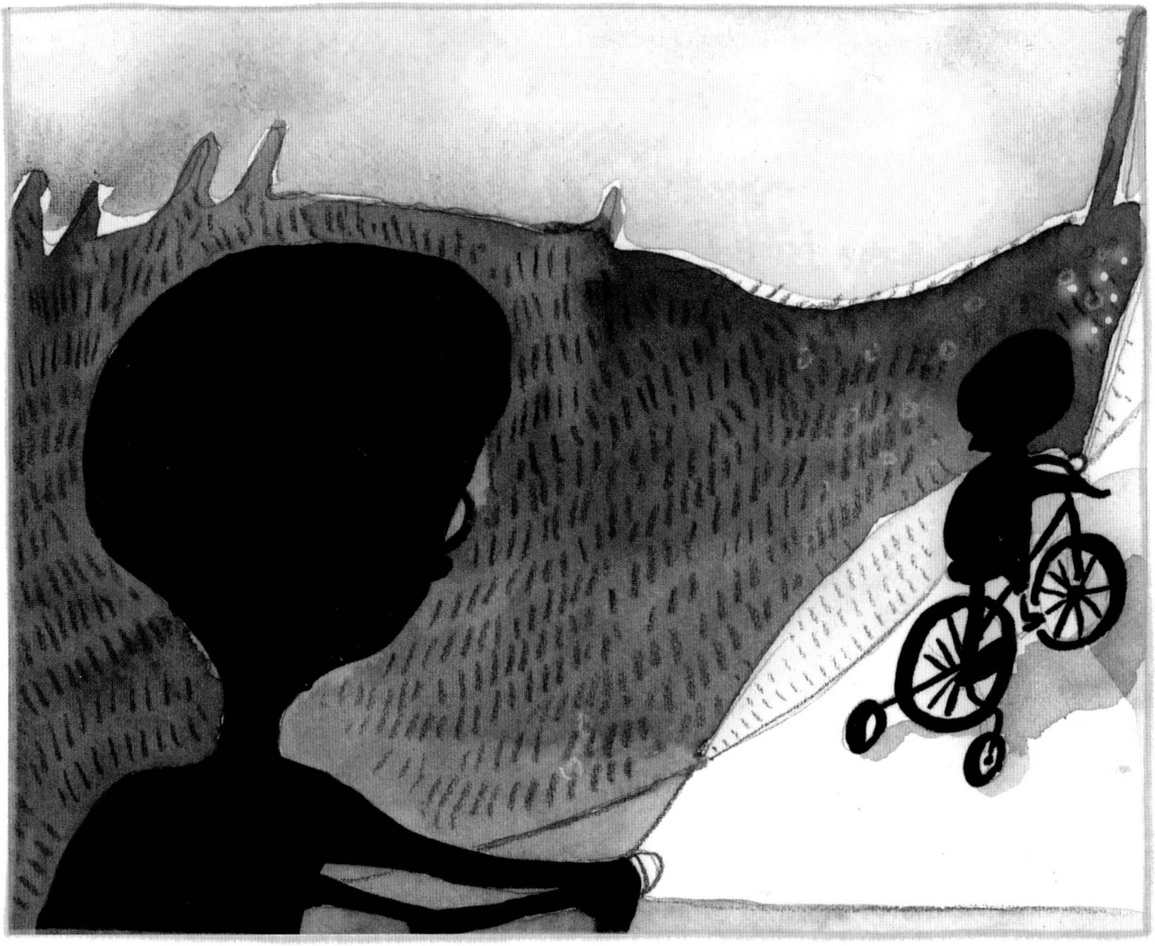

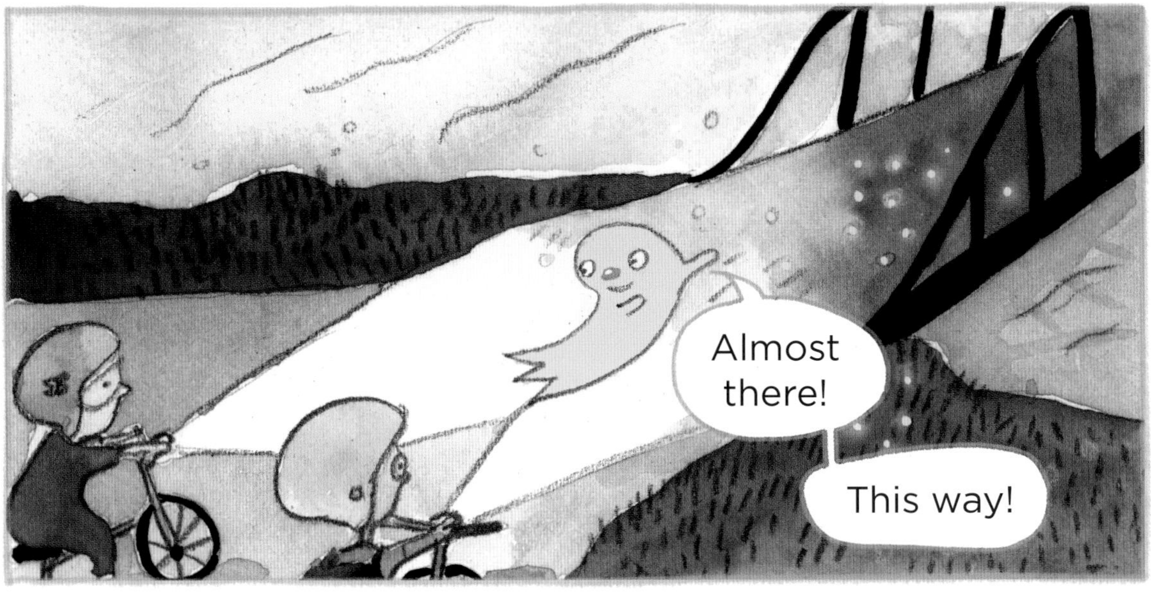
Almost there!
This way!

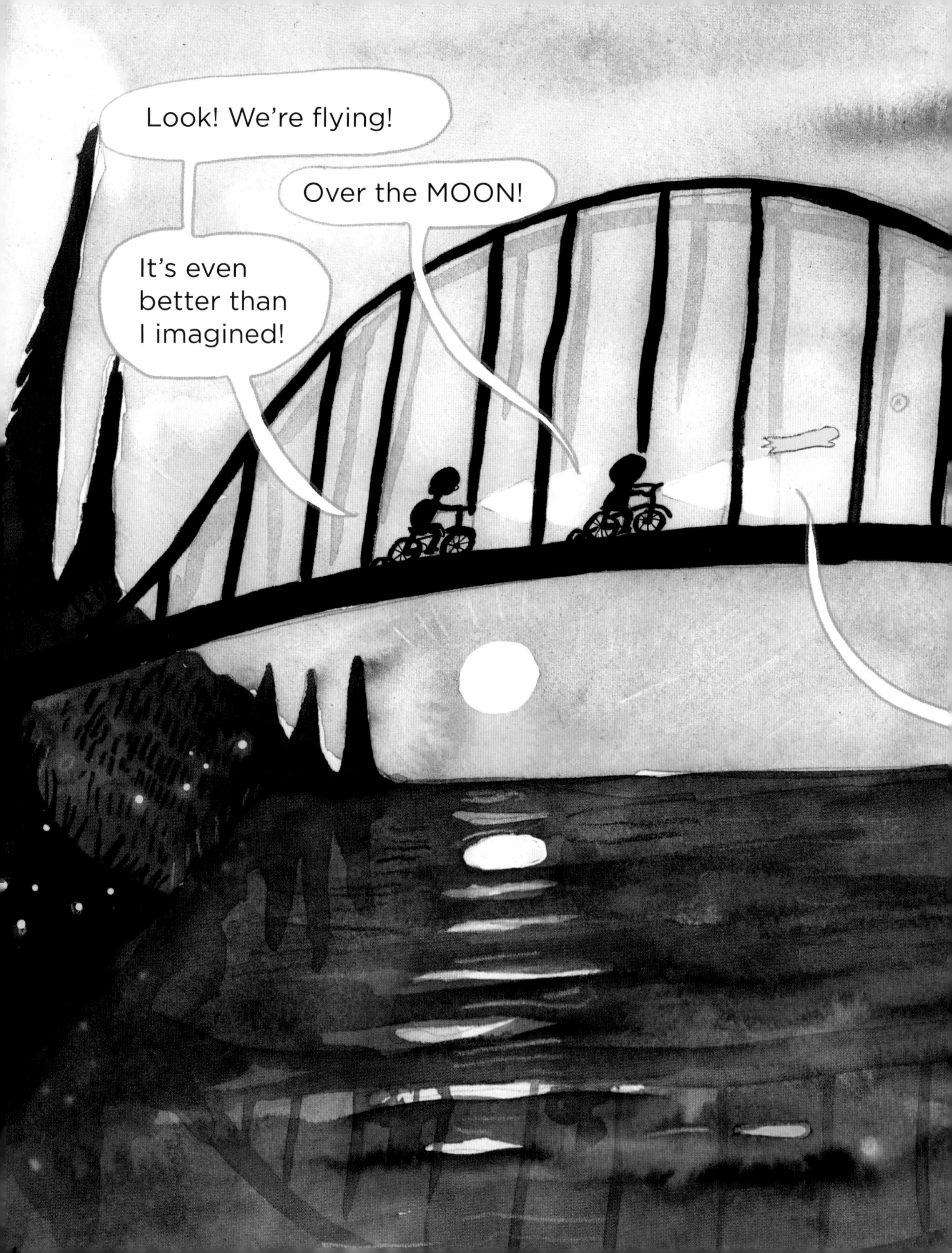
Look! We're flying!
Over the MOON!
It's even better than I imagined!

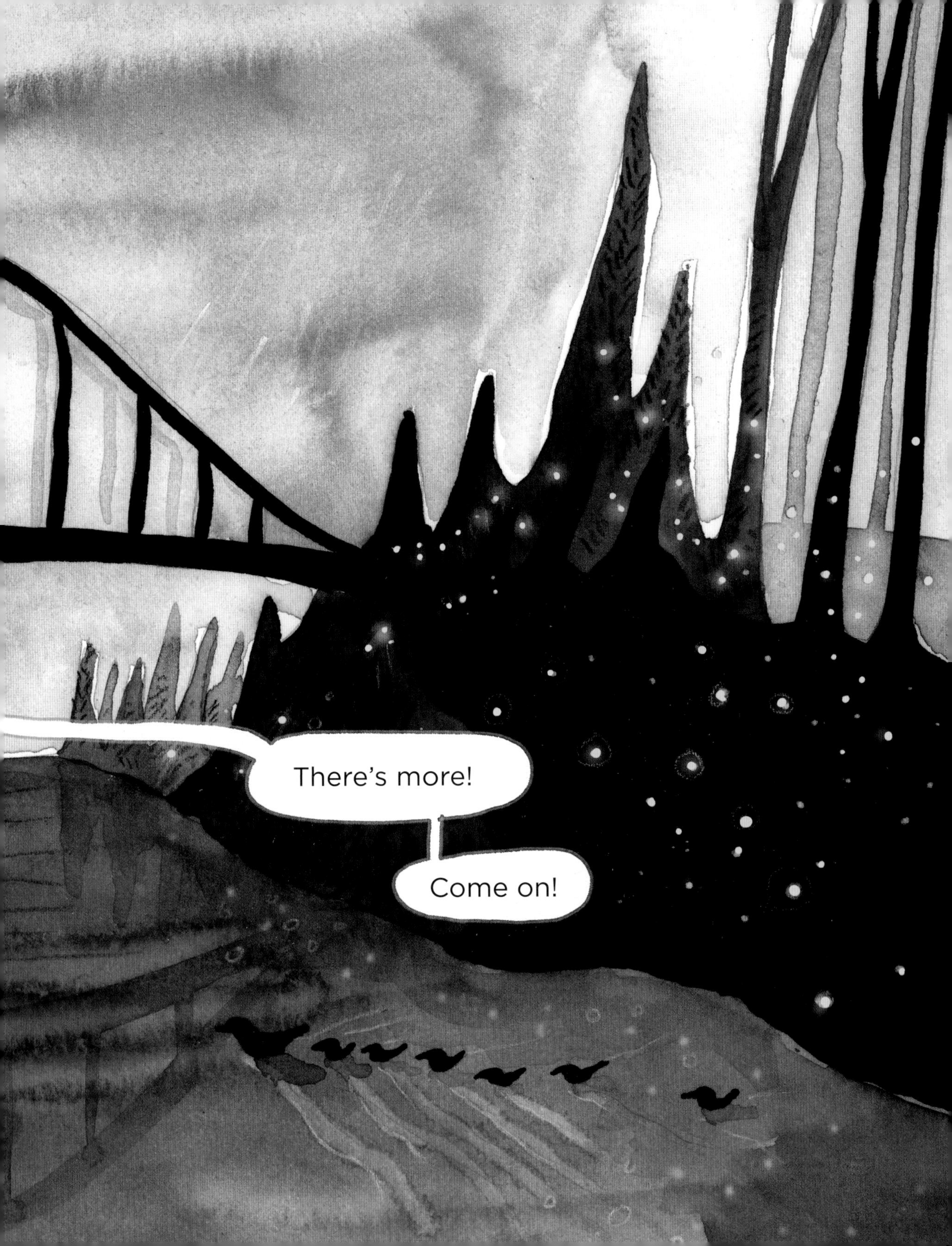
There's more!
Come on!

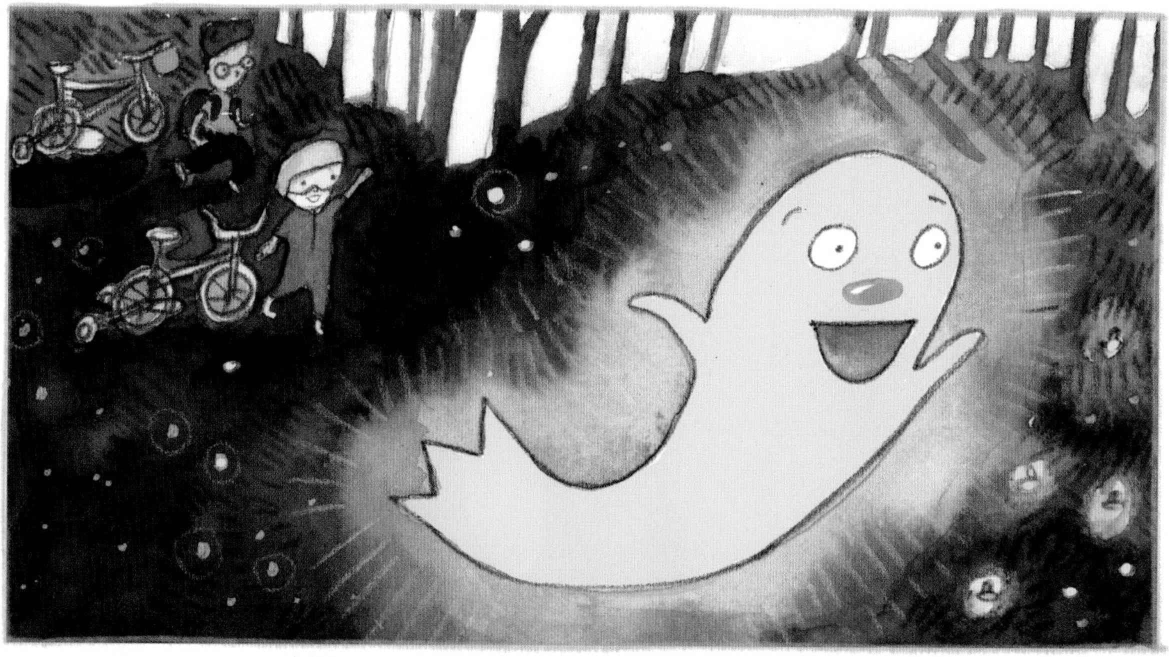

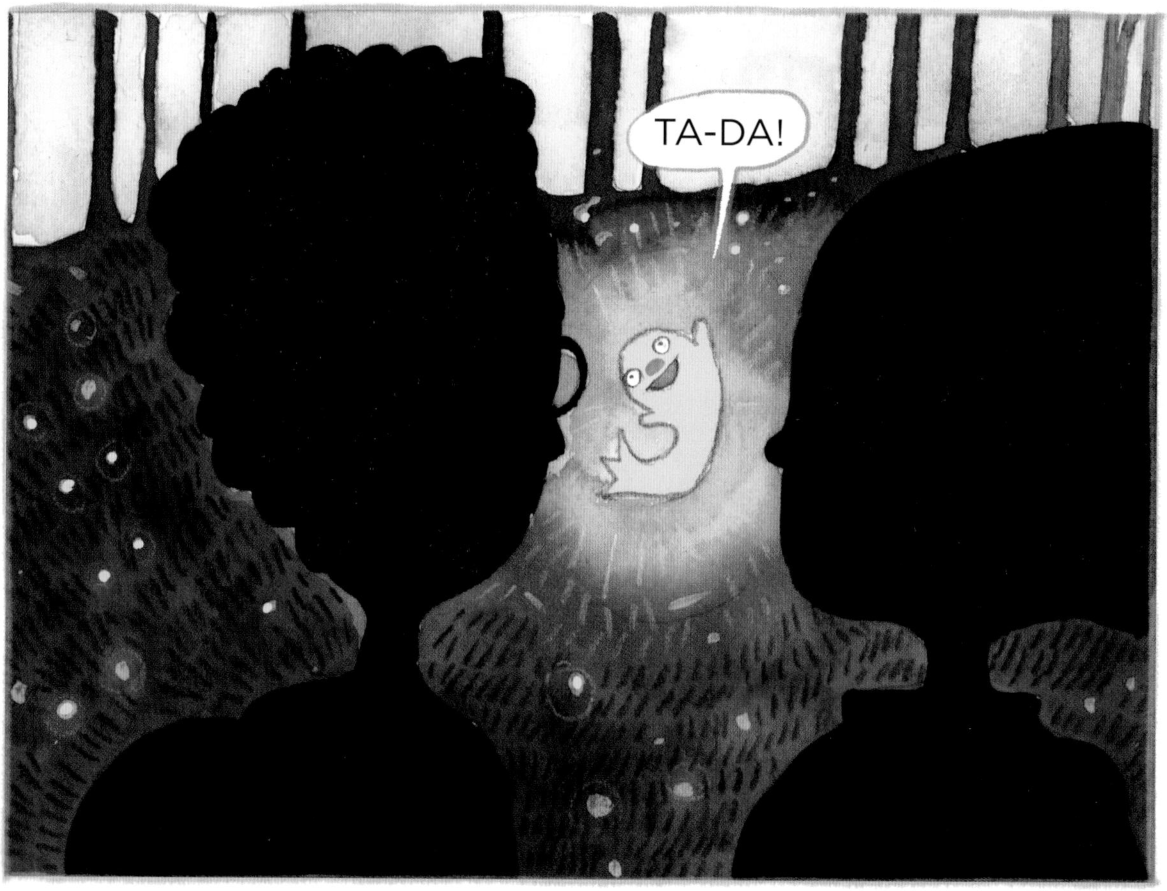
TA-DA!

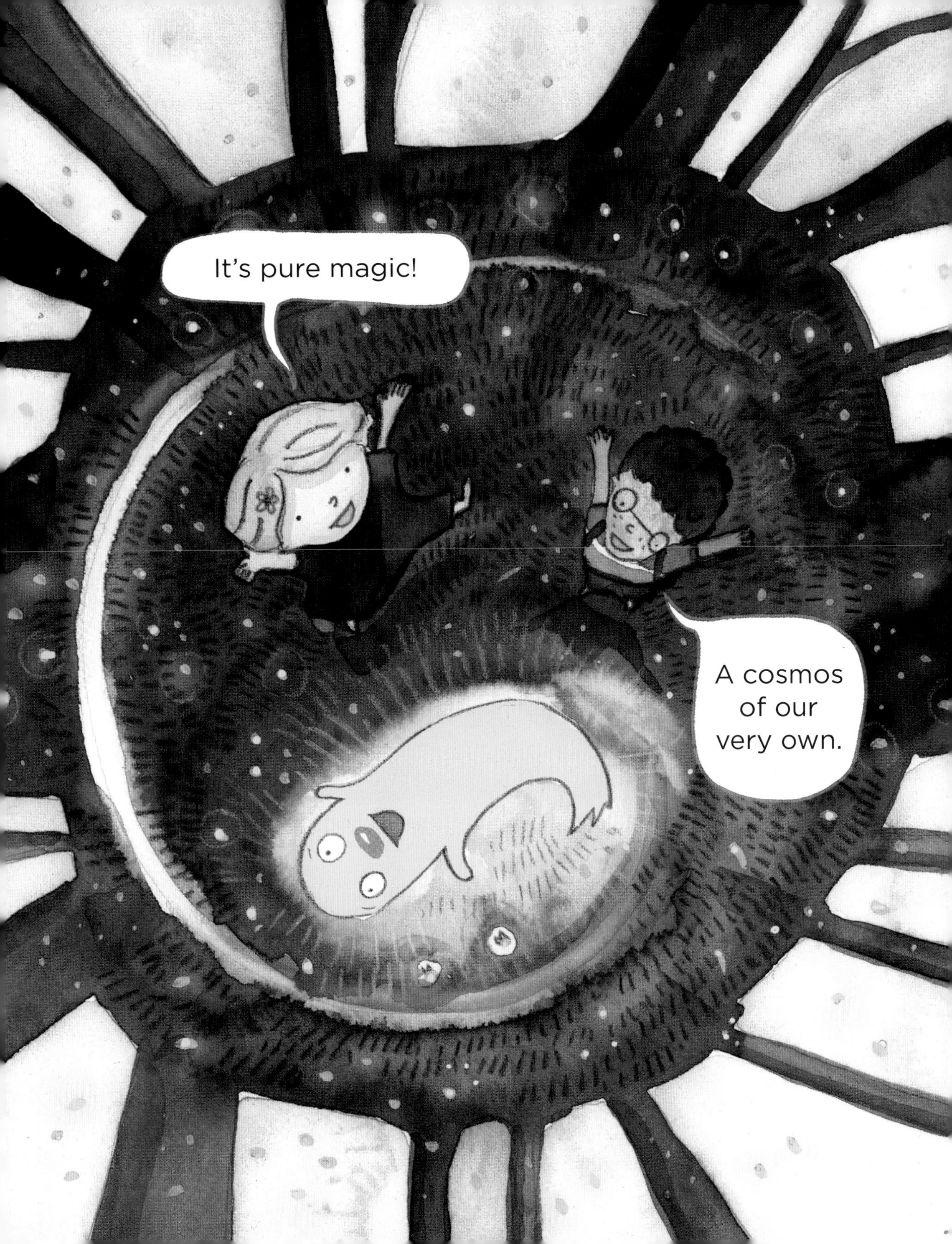
It’s pure magic!
A cosmos of our very own.

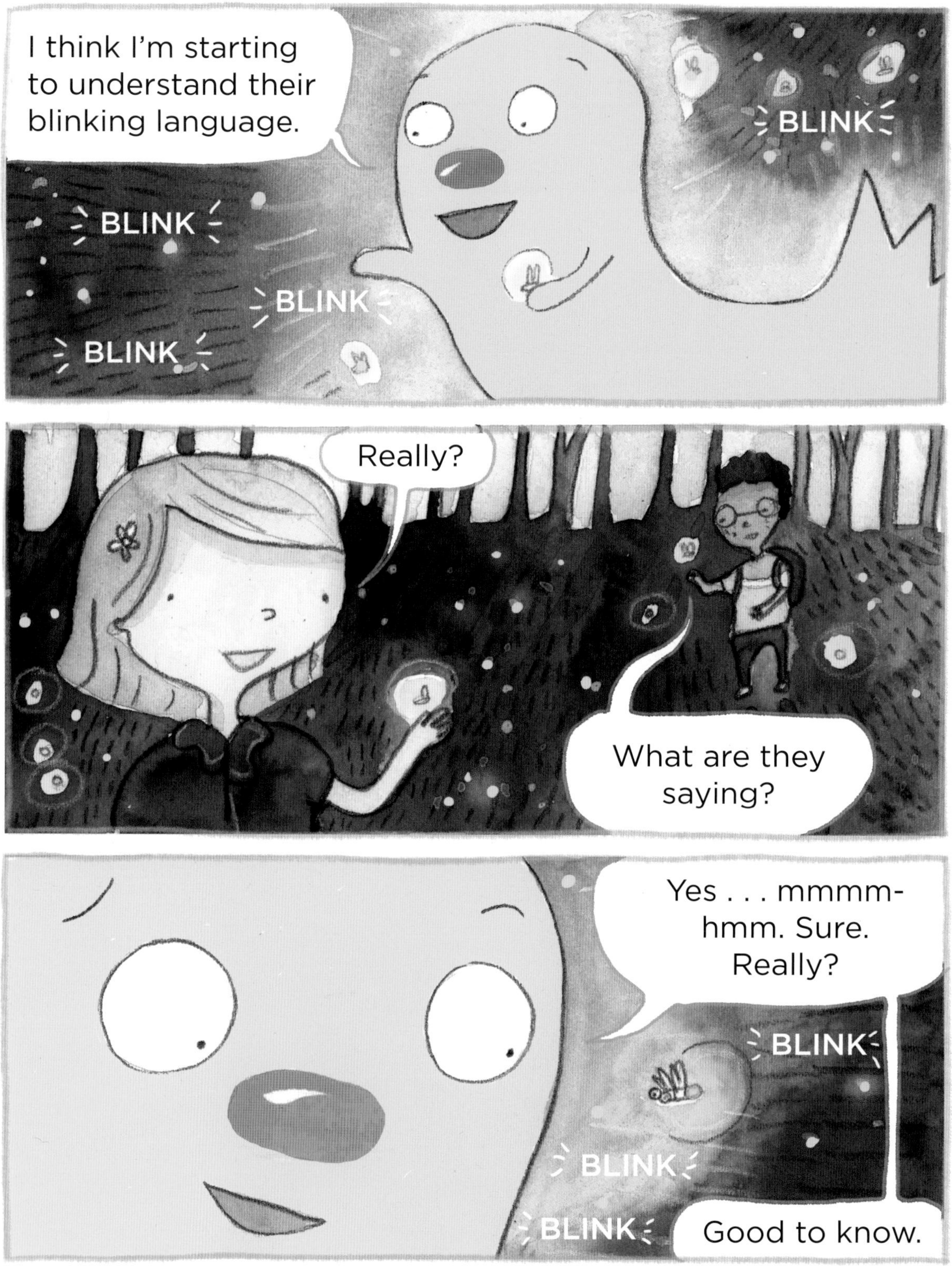
I think I'm starting to understand their blinking language.
BLINK
BLINK
BLINK
BLINK
BLINK
Really?
What are they saying?
Yes . . . mmmm-hmm. Sure. Really?
BLINK
BLINK
BLINK
Good to know.

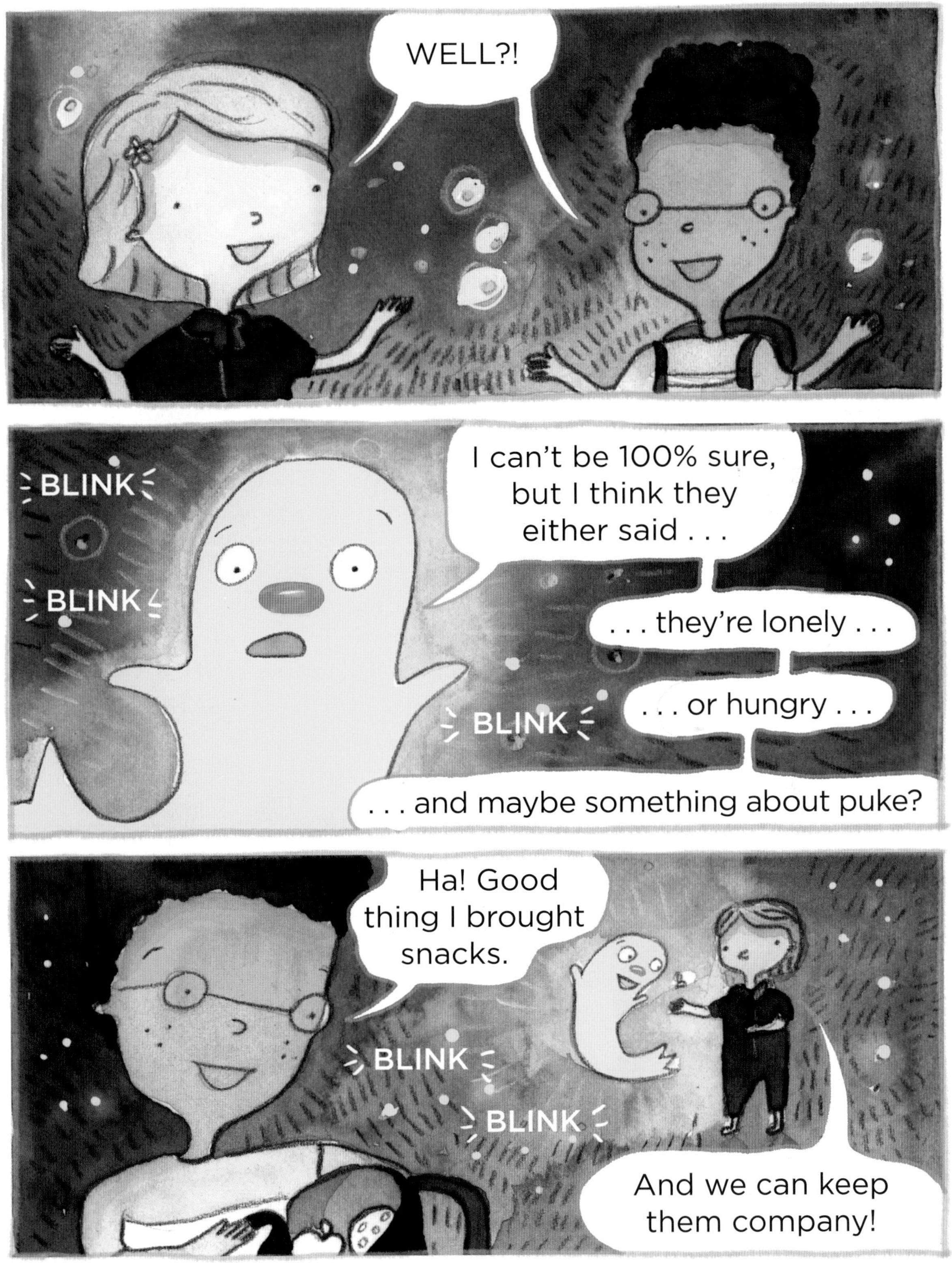
WELL?!
BLINK
BLINK
I can't be 100% sure, but I think they either said . . .
. . . they're lonely . . .
. . . or hungry . . .
BLINK
. . . and maybe something about puke?
Ha! Good thing I brought snacks.
BLINK
BLINK
And we can keep them company!

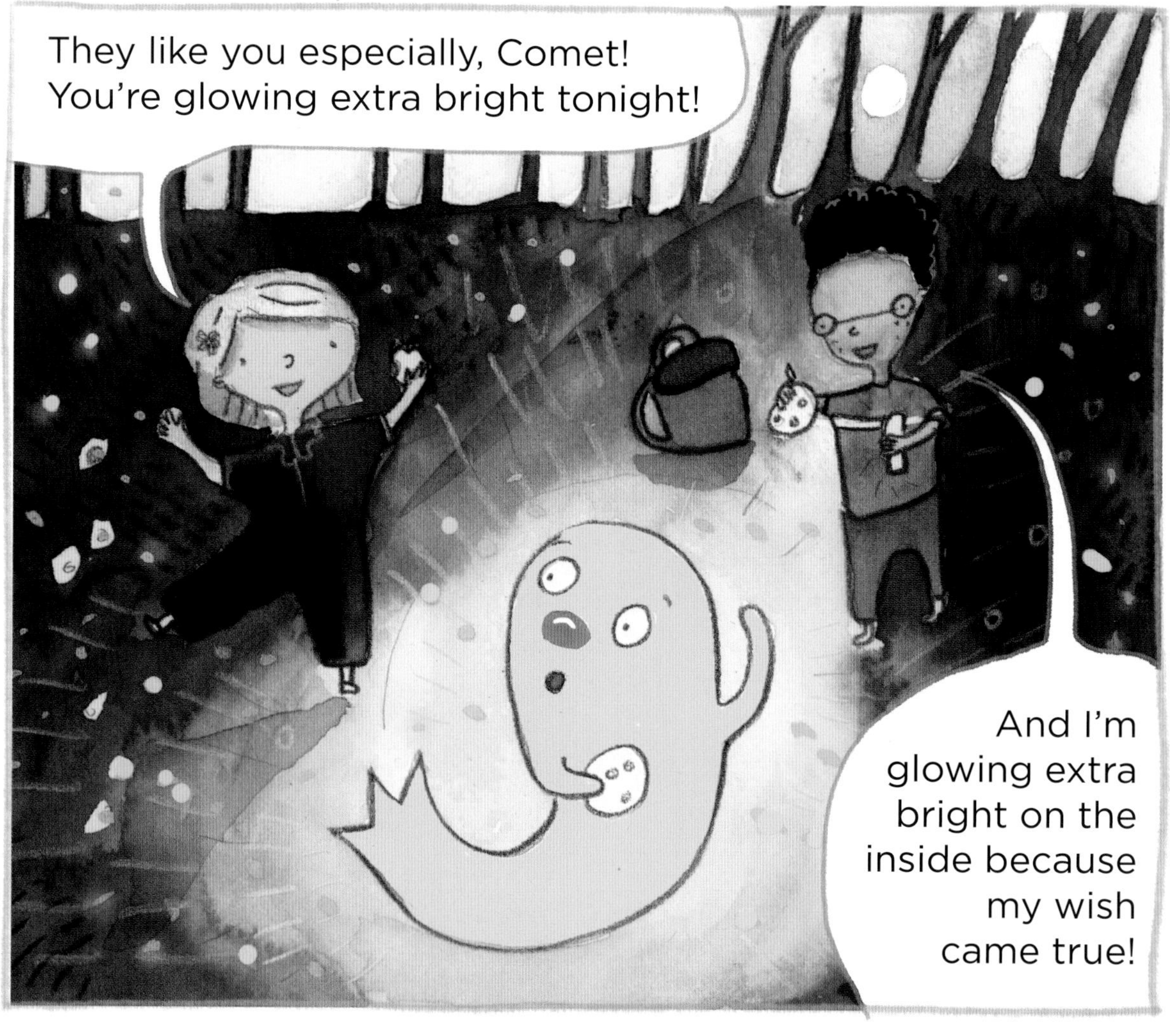
They like you especially, Comet! You're glowing extra bright tonight!
And I'm glowing extra bright on the inside because my wish came true!

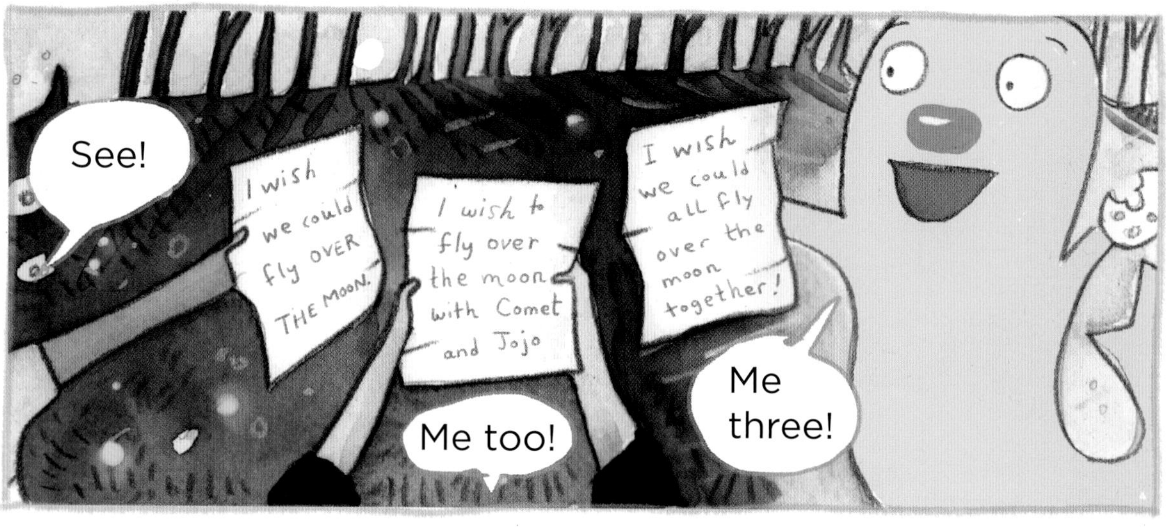
See!
I wish we could fly OVER THE MOON.
I wish to fly over the moon with Comet and Jojo
I wish we could all fly over the moon together!
Me too!
Me three!

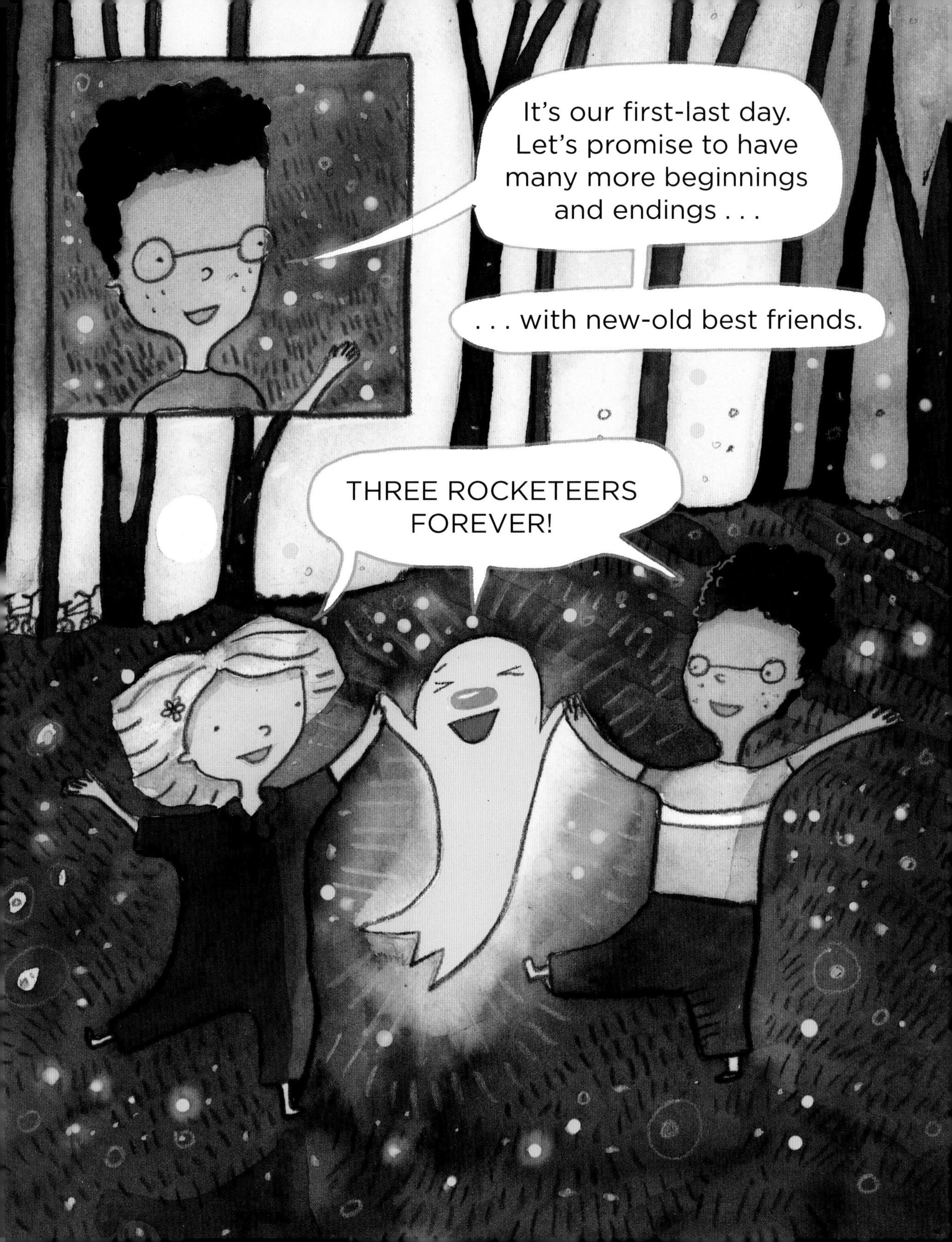
It's our first-last day. Let's promise to have many more beginnings and endings . . .
. . . with new-old best friends.
THREE ROCKETEERS FOREVER!

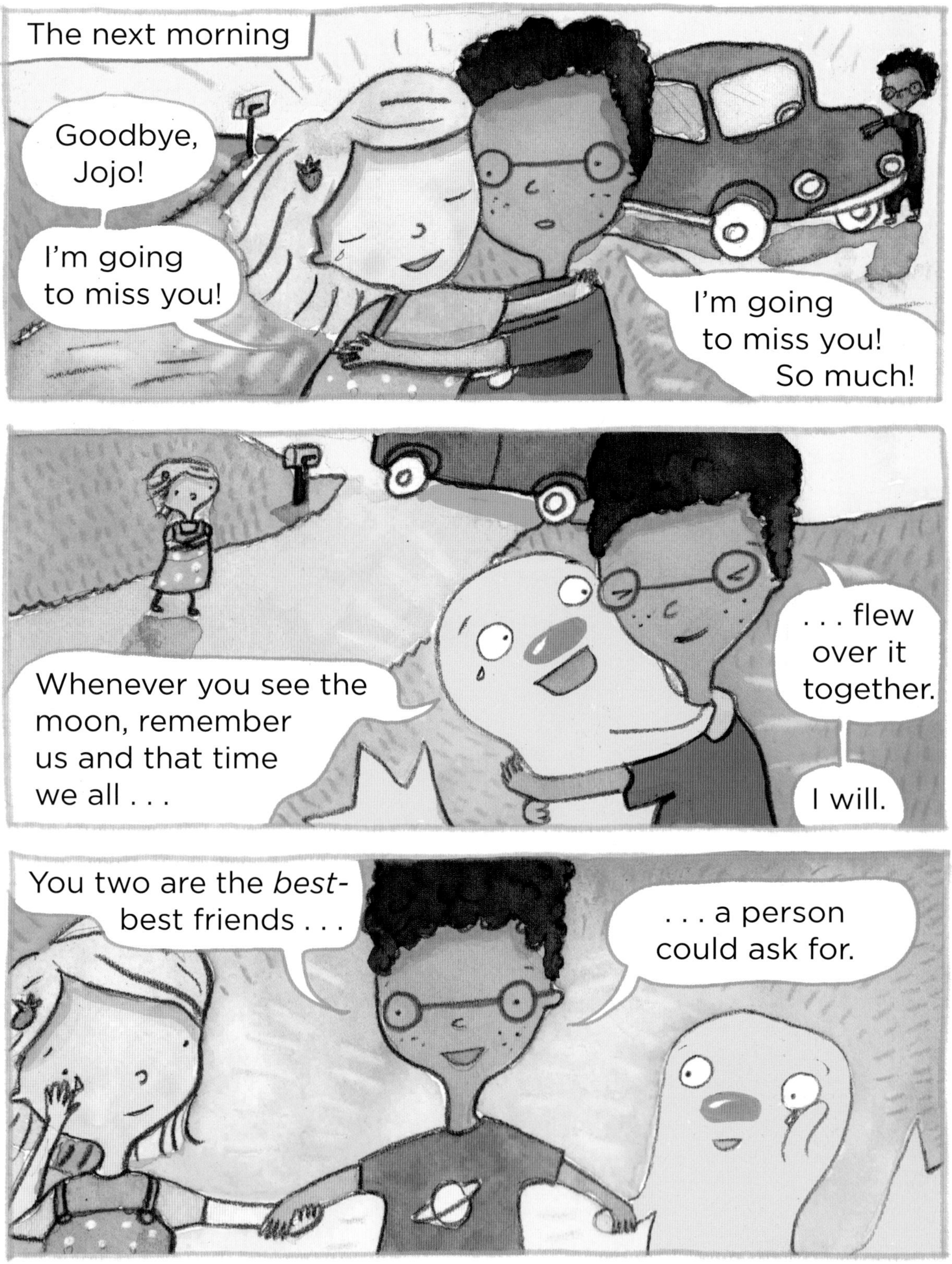
The next morning
Goodbye, Jojo!
I'm going to miss you!
I'm going to miss you! So much!
Whenever you see the moon, remember us and that time we all . . .
. . . flew over it together.
I will.
You two are the *best*-best friends . . .
. . . a person could ask for.

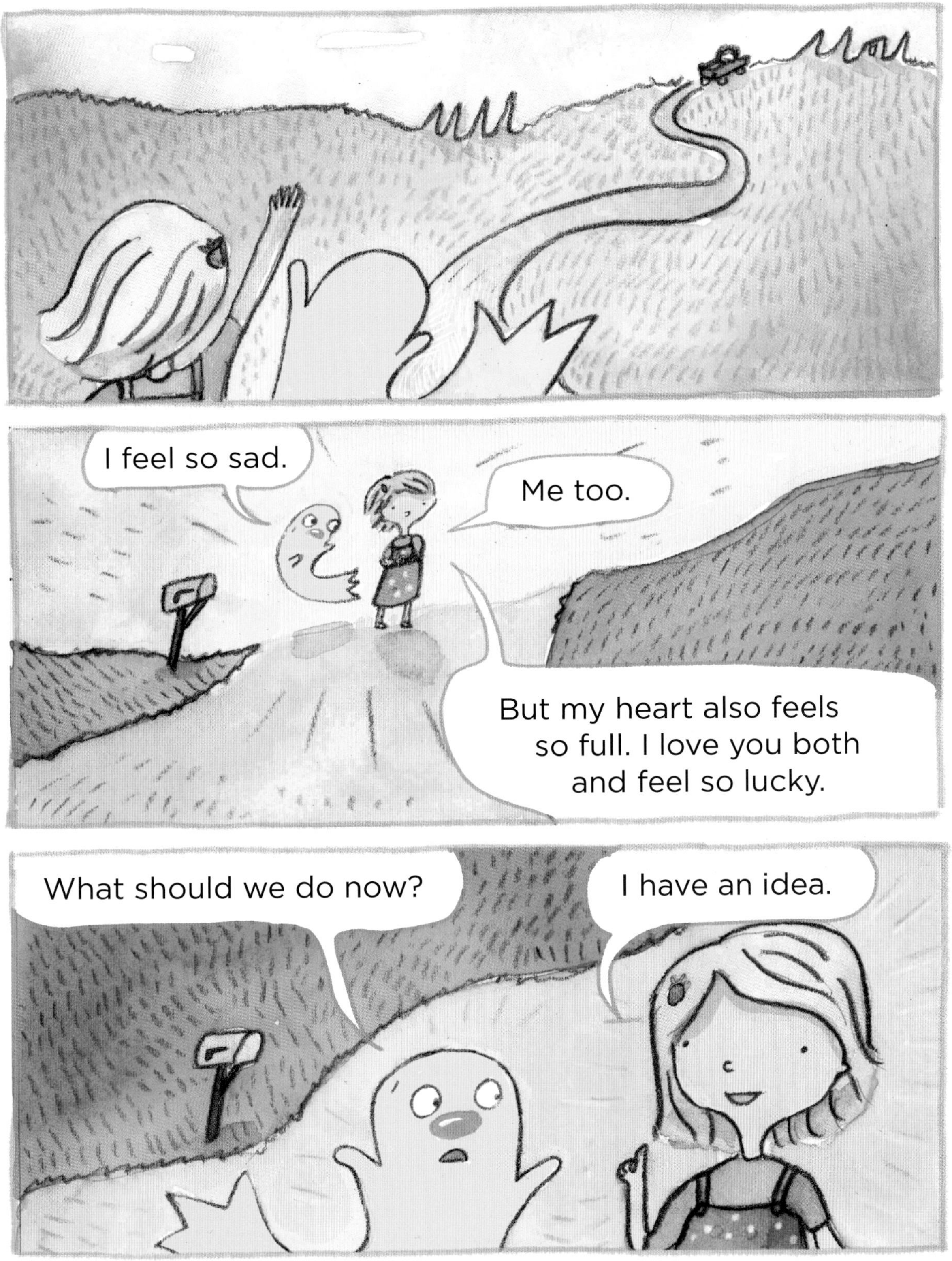
I feel so sad.
Me too.
But my heart also feels so full. I love you both and feel so lucky.
What should we do now?
I have an idea.

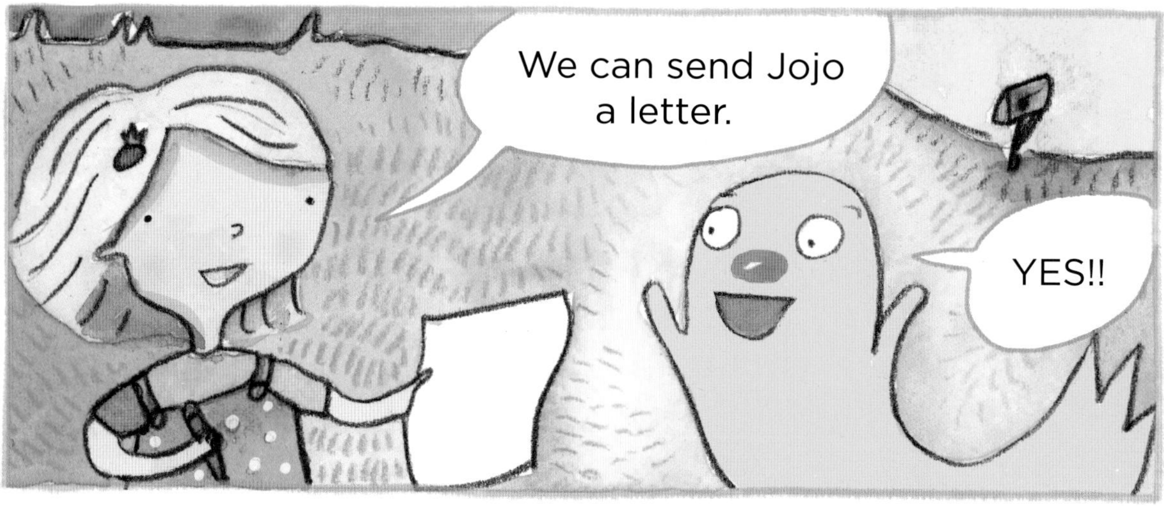
We can send Jojo a letter.
YES!!

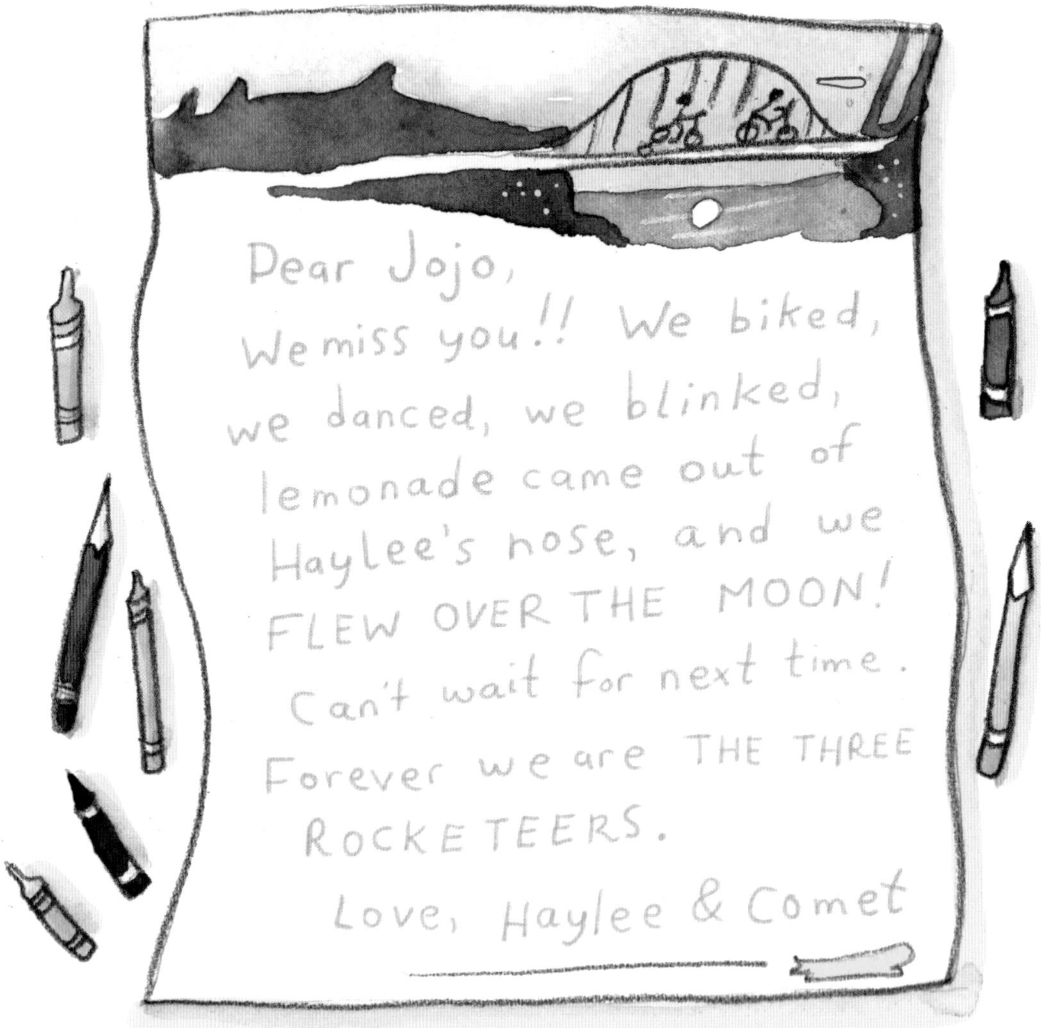
Dear Jojo,
We miss you!! We biked, we danced, we blinked, lemonade came out of Haylee's nose, and we FLEW OVER THE MOON!
Can't wait for next time.
Forever we are THE THREE ROCKETEERS.
Love, Haylee & Comet

It really is like a portal.

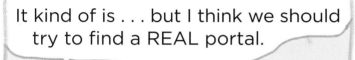

It kind of is . . . but I think we should try to find a REAL portal.

One both of us can fit through.

What are we waiting for?

LET'S GO!

## **EXTRA!** HAYLEE AND COMET INTERVIEW THE MOON!

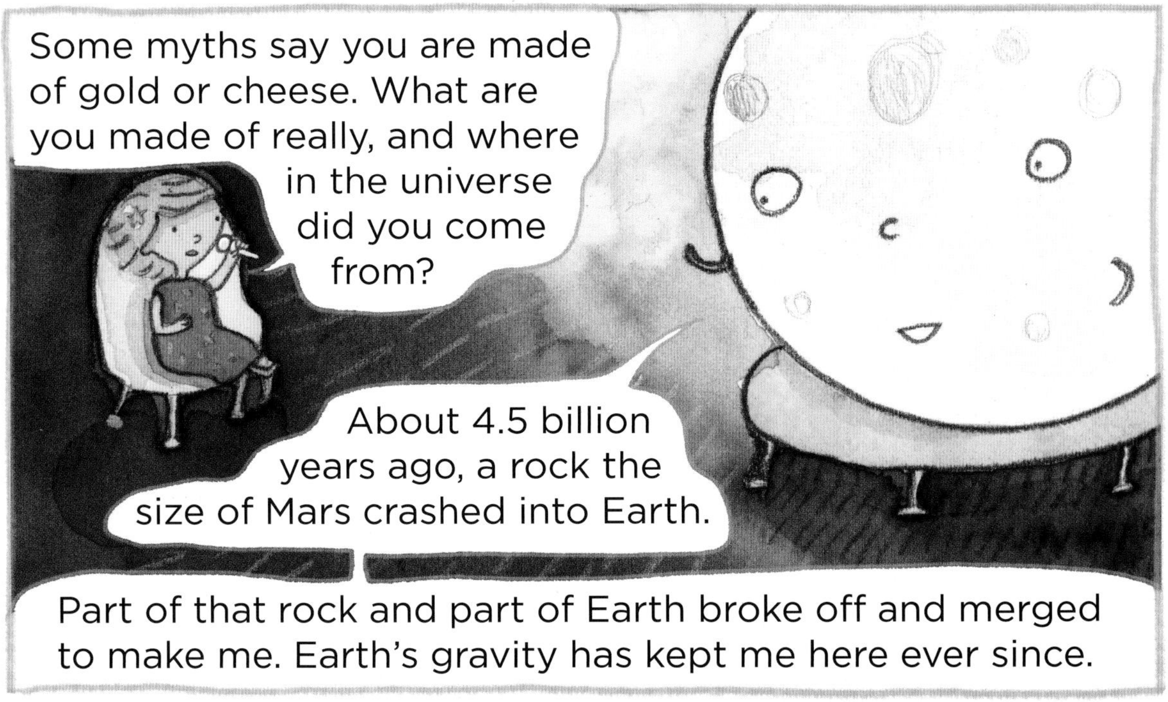
Some myths say you are made of gold or cheese. What are you made of really, and where in the universe did you come from?
About 4.5 billion years ago, a rock the size of Mars crashed into Earth.
Part of that rock and part of Earth broke off and merged to make me. Earth's gravity has kept me here ever since.

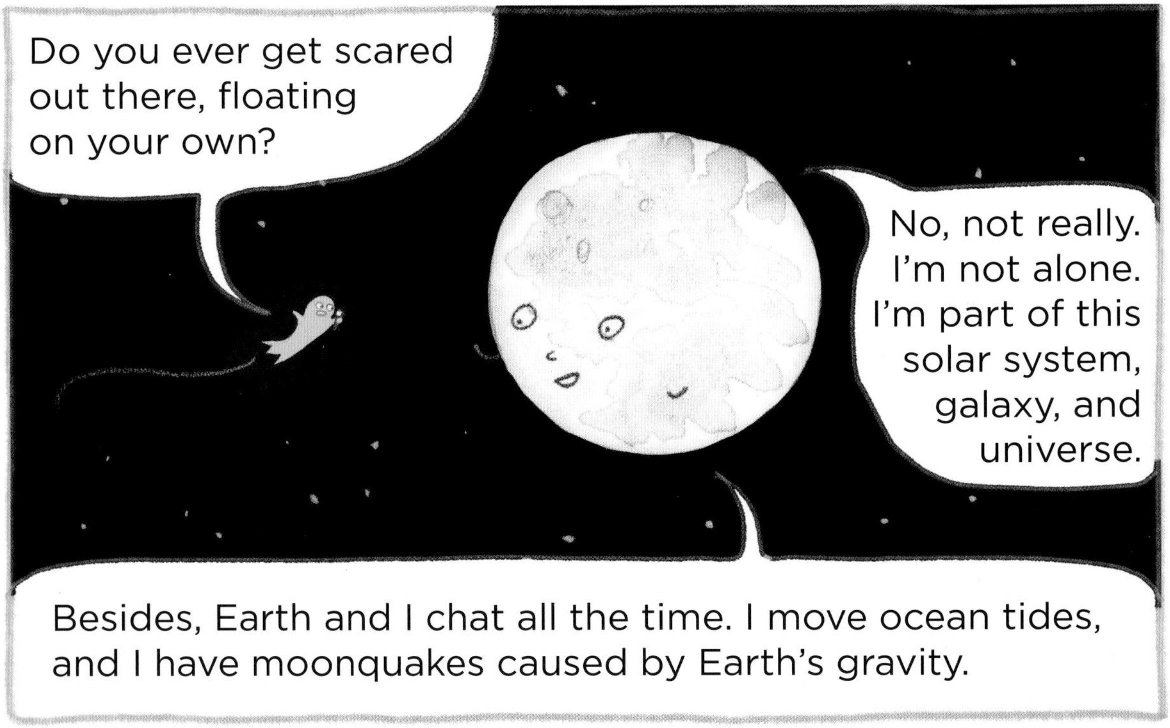
Do you ever get scared out there, floating on your own?
No, not really. I'm not alone. I'm part of this solar system, galaxy, and universe.
Besides, Earth and I chat all the time. I move ocean tides, and I have moonquakes caused by Earth's gravity.

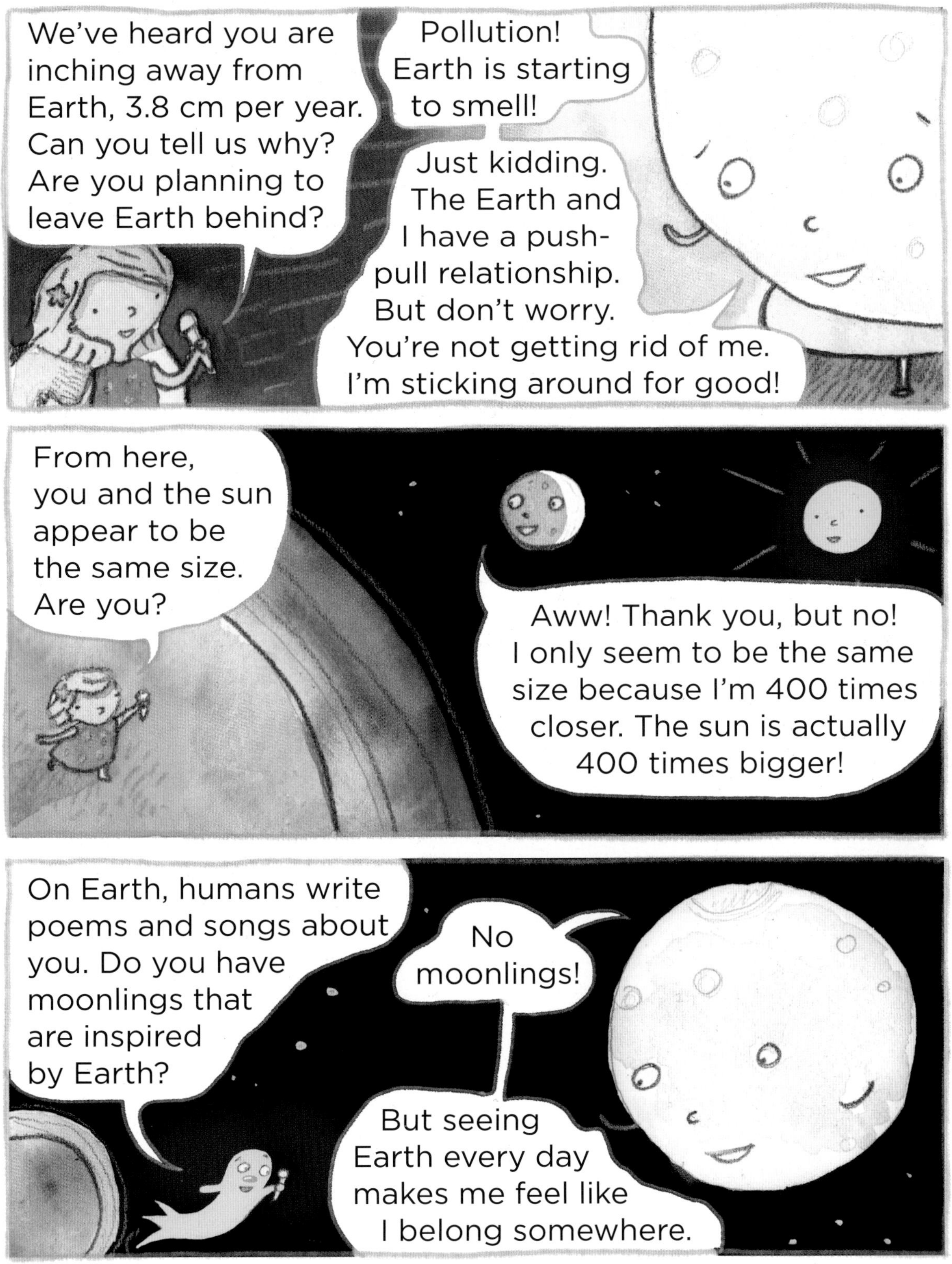
We've heard you are inching away from Earth, 3.8 cm per year. Can you tell us why? Are you planning to leave Earth behind?
Pollution! Earth is starting to smell!
Just kidding. The Earth and I have a push-pull relationship. But don't worry. You're not getting rid of me. I'm sticking around for good!
From here, you and the sun appear to be the same size. Are you?
Aww! Thank you, but no! I only seem to be the same size because I'm 400 times closer. The sun is actually 400 times bigger!
On Earth, humans write poems and songs about you. Do you have moonlings that are inspired by Earth?
No moonlings!
But seeing Earth every day makes me feel like I belong somewhere.